Among the more il  P9-DNZ-246
at the Saints-Cowboys game were:

**HIS ROYAL HIGHNESS SHEIKH ABDUL-
LAH BEN ABZUG:** The sheikh's English was
limited to a few pleasantries such as "Up
yours!" and "Your mother wears army boots"
—greetings he bestowed on everyone he met.

LANCE FAIRBANKS and his friend BRUCIE:
They were proud owners of the only lavender
Winnebago camper in the West. It had, among
other things, a doorbell that chimed "Tiptoe
Through the Tulips."

IDA-SUE DALRYMPLE: A former University
of Texas pom pom girl, she had long ago
offered her "pearl of great price" to her future
husband, Congressman Davy Crockett "Alamo" Jones. This she had done in the back seat
of the convertible given to her by her adoring
Daddy.

"BUBBA" BURTON: Known as Pigman to all
the C.B.'ers back in Carolina, Bubba finally
heard heavenly music when he met Ida-Sue's
voluptuous daughter, Scarlett.

TEDDY ROOSEVELT: A splendid specimen
of *Bison Americanus*, Teddy had the distinct
honor of owning a genuine American cowboy
and an Indian chief.

Books in the MASH Series

Published by POCKET BOOKS

M*A*S*H
Goes to Texas

Richard Hooker
and
William E. Butterworth

A KANGAROO BOOK
PUBLISHED BY POCKET BOOKS NEW YORK

MASH GOES TO TEXAS

POCKET BOOK edition published February, 1977

This original POCKET BOOK edition is printed from brand-new
plates made from newly set, clear, easy-to-read type.
POCKET BOOK editions are published by
POCKET BOOKS,
a division of Simon & Schuster, Inc.,
A GULF+WESTERN COMPANY
630 Fifth Avenue,
New York, N.Y. 10020.
Trademarks registered in the United States
and other countries.

ISBN: 0-671-80892-3.

Printed in the U.S.A.

In fond memory of
Malcolm Reiss,
gentleman literary agent
June 3, 1905–December 17, 1975
—Richard Hooker
and W. E. Butterworth

M★A★S★H

Goes to Texas

Chapter One

Truth to tell, T. Alfred Crumley, Sr., administrator
of the Spruce Harbor, Maine, Medical Center, who
happened to be of the Roman Catholic persuasion,
privately regarded Benjamin Franklin Pierce, M.D.,
F.A.C.S., who did not happen to be of the Roman
Catholic persuasion, as a fire-breathing heathen.

Dr. Pierce, who was the chief of surgery, had, it
must in honesty be related, not done very much to
disabuse Mr. Crumley of his belief. Quite the con-
trary, in fact. Secretly aided and abetted by his longtime crony, the co-proprietor of the Finest Kind Fish
Market and Medical Clinic, John Francis Xavier Mc-
Intyre, M.D., F.A.C.S., who, although he himself was
a Roman Catholic in more or less good standing,
shared Dr. Pierce's belief that T. Alfred Crumley, Sr.,
was a prime example of the southern end of a north-
bound horse, Dr. Pierce had arranged for Mr. Crumley
to come upon him, prior to a surgical procedure, en-

gaged in what looked like the celebration of an obscene pagan rite.

Actually, there were three co-conspirators, the other two also adherents of the Roman Catholic faith. Esther Flanagan, R.N., Chief of Nursing Services, had, demonstrating a high level of skill with needle and thread, come up with the hooded black robe and personally designed the pagan symbols with which she liberally adorned, in sequins, the back of the robe.

Stanley K. Warczinski, Sr., proprietor of the Bide-a-While Pool Hall/Ladies Served Fresh Lobsters & Clams Daily Restaurant and Saloon, Inc., had contributed the moose head and wildcat. Both of these items were stuffed, of course, and usually decorated Mr. Warczinski's place of business. He also contributed a very large and freshly boiled lobster and a raw, plucked chicken.

Mr. T. Alfred Crumley had received a telephone call from Nurse Flanagan, asking him to investigate the strange noises coming from a room designated as the female surgeons' locker room.

Mr. Crumley had been quick to do his duty and investigate. There was no surgeon of the female variety on the Spruce Harbor medical staff, and thus the locker room in question was unused.

Mr. Crumley had paused outside the female surgeons' locker room when he pressed his ear to the door so that he might hear whatever was going on in there. His face had paled when a most horrifying sound came through the door. It instantly gave him visions of the hereafter as depicted by Dante. What he heard was music, or at least a profane, indecent, and horrifying kind of music, discordant, mournful and blood-chilling.*

---

* What this was was a tape recording of Fred Waring's Pennsylvanians singing "I Want a Girl—Just Like the Girl That Married Dear Old Dad," played backward and at a very slow speed.

He gathered his courage and, sweating clammily, he pushed open the door. A chain lock kept the door from opening more than a crack, but there was enough room for T. Alfred Crumley to press his eye to the crack and see what was going on inside.

He recoiled in shock and horror, closing his eyes in a futile attempt to wipe from his brain what he had seen. Then, shivering, he looked again. His eyes had not fooled him; what he had seen before he saw again.

Crossing himself in what he hoped was a gesture of exorcism, he considered his next step of action. And then he rushed down the corridor to report this outrageous circumstance to his superior, the chief of staff.

"What is it, Crumley?" that distinguished healer asked. "You look as if you've just seen a ghost."

"Worse!" Mr. Crumley said. "Much worse!"

"Stop babbling, Crumley, and get to the point."

"I don't know how to tell you this, Doctor," Mr. Crumley said, "but the thing is, Dr. Pierce is celebrating a black mass in the female surgeons' locker room."

"You want to let me have that again, Crumley?" the chief of staff said. "It sounded for a moment like you said that Hawkeye* was celebrating a black mass in the female surgeons' locker room."

"That's what I said!" Crumley said. "That's what I said!"

The chief of staff moved very close to Mr. Crumley, close enough to get a good sniff of his breath. He couldn't smell anything, but he realized that vodka is generally odorless.

"You don't say?" he said, remembering from his courses in psychiatry that it is a good idea never to

---

* Dr. Pierce's father was a great fan of James Fenimore Cooper. He wished to name his firstborn after Cooper's character, the Indian brave, Hawkeye. Mrs. Pierce prevailed at christening time, but Mr. Pierce was undaunted. He never called his little Benjamin anything but Hawkeye, and the name stuck.

argue with a nut, no matter how absurd a pronounce-ment the nut makes. "What makes you think so?"

"I don't think you believe me, Doctor!" Mr. Crumley said, right on the edge of hysteria.

"Why don't you just tell me what you saw, Mr. Crumley?"

"I'll tell you what I saw," Mr. Crumley said. "What I saw was Dr. Pierce—in a hooded black robe."

"Really?"

"With all kinds of pagan symbols on it," Crumley went on.

"How interesting!"

"*Shocking* is a better word," Crumley said.

"And what was he doing?"

"There were flickering candles and an *awful* smell of incense!" Crumley said.

"I see. And was Dr. Pierce doing anything un-usual?"

"Was he ever!"

"What, specifically?"

"There was a wildcat in there with him," Crumley said.

"You don't say?"

"Standing up on his hind legs and snarling," Crum-ley amplified.

"How interesting! But what was Dr. Pierce doing that makes you think he was celebrating a black mass?"

"I'll tell you what he was doing," Crumley said. "With his right hand he was feeding a dead chicken to the wildcat; and with the other hand he was feeding a lobster to a moose head!"

"Well, now," the chief of staff replied. "Why don't we just go take a look?"

By the time the chief of staff and Mr. Crumley got back to the female surgeons' locker room, of course, the chicken and lobster had been taken to the kitchen; the moose head and the stuffed wildcat had been sent on their way back to Bide-a-While in the custody of Mr. Warczinski; and the sole occupant of the room was Esther Flanagan, R.N., Chief of Nursing Services.

She turned around from examining her coiffure in the mirror when Mr. Crumley flung the door open and announced, "See for yourself, Doctor!"

"Shame on you, Mr. Crumley!" Nurse Flanagan said rather indignantly. "How dare you burst in here like that!"

"I won't go into detail, Nurse Flanagan," the chief of staff said. "I'll just ask you, as senior member of our staff, to trust me. I'm afraid Mr. Crumley has been under a good deal of pressure lately."

"Where's Dr. Pierce?" Mr. Crumley demanded. "Where's Dr. Pierce?"

"I would suppose that he's in the other locker room," Nurse Flanagan replied. "What made you think he'd be in here?"

"I saw him in here, that's why!" Mr. Crumley replied.

"I hardly think that's possible," Nurse Flanagan replied.

The chief of staff winked at Nurse Flanagan.

"Tell her what you saw him doing, Mr. Crumley," he said.

"He was feeding a lobster to a moose head—*that's* what he was doing!"

"Poor Mr. Crumley," Nurse Flanagan said, oozing professional and feminine sympathy from every pore. "I guess he has been working too hard."

When he had time to think about it* over the next

---

* Mr. Crumley was immediately placed on two weeks' sick leave by the chief of staff, a circumstance that took something—not much, but something—from the feeling of sweet triumph shared by Drs. Pierce and McIntyre and Nurse Flanagan.

two weeks, Mr. Crumley came to understand what had happened. The insight came after U.P.S. delivered a small brown box containing the hooded black robe. He had been made a fool of. He was smart enough to realize that he would look like even more of a fool if he carried the robe to the chief of staff. He was even smart enough to conclude (correctly) that this was Hawkeye's intention in sending him the robe. The chief of staff would believe, when he rushed to show him the "proof," that he had had the robe made up to prove his story. He would look even worse.

So he burned the robe and said nothing, not even when he stopped by Bide-a-While for a cold beer and saw the wildcat and the moose head in their usual positions above the bar. There was an explanation for the whole thing. Dr. Benjamin Franklin Pierce was a heathen. Only a heathen would be capable of thinking up something like that, and only a fire-breathing heathen would be capable of carrying it out. Mr. Crumley took what solace he could from his belief in what would happen to Dr. Pierce in the hereafter. Dr. Hawkeye Pierce would get what heathens got, and double.

Among Dr. Pierce's many other annoying habits was what Mr. Crumley considered his severe case of telephonitis. Whenever he wished to ask someone something, or tell someone something, he thought absolutely nothing about picking up the telephone and calling them, no matter where they might be. Not only did this run up the hospital's telephone bill outrageously, but it deprived Mr. Crumley's staff of typists and file clerks of their right to type letters, and file copies of same, together with replies, if any.

Mr. Crumley's weekly litany of complaints about the telephoning to the chief of staff finally bore fruit.

At a brief little conference held as Dr. Pierce was about to leave the hospital for Bide-a-While, Dr. Pierce promised the chief of staff faithfully, with Crumley standing there as a witness, that he would henceforth and forever more call long distance only in cases of absolute necessity, and that he would pay for personal calls himself.

It was hours later before Mr. Crumley realized that Dr. Pierce would be the judge of what was an "absolutely necessary" telephone call, and that things were, and would be, unchanged in these circumstances. He then decided it was not only his right, but his clear duty, to "monitor" Dr. Pierce's long-distance telephony.

He issued strict orders that whenever Dr. Pierce placed a long-distance call, he was to be notified of all the details, and immediately.

And so it came to pass that Mr. Crumley became a silent listener to a telephone call placed to New Orleans, Louisiana. It began when his own telephone rang.

"Office of the hospital administrator," he said, "T. Alfred Crumley, Sr., speaking."

"Crumbum," Hazel, the telephone operator, said, "violating my sense of right and wrong, I'm reporting that Hawkeye just put in a call to New Orleans."

"That's *'Mr.* Crum*ley'* and 'Dr. Pierce,' Hazel," he corrected her. He realized at that point that she had hung up on him. Pursing his lips in displeasure, he got her back on the line.

"To whom, Hazel, did Hawkeye place the call?"

"That's 'Dr. Pierce' to you, Crumbum," Hazel said. "The call is to Reverend Mother Superior Bernadette of Lourdes."

"To whom?" What, wondered Mr. Crumley, would a fire-breathing heathen be up to by placing a call to a party whose name suggested she was a distinguished religious of the Church?

"Reverend Mother Superior Bernadette of Lourdes," Hazel replied.

Mr. Crumley dropped his phone in its cradle and rushed to the switchboard, where he picked up a headset and punched the appropriate buttons so that he could, as he thought of it, "monitor" the conversation.

"Lousy eavesdropper," Hazel said in something louder than a whisper. Mr. Crumley ignored her.

"Gates of Heaven Hospital," an operator said.

"Dr. B. F. Pierce calling for Reverend Mother Superior Bernadette of Lourdes," Hazel said.

"One moment, operator. I'll see if I can find the Reverend Mother," the operator said. Another voice came on the line.

"The Reverend Mother's office, Sister Piety speaking."

"Dr. Pierce for the Reverend Mother," the operator said.

"She's in conference, operator," Sister Piety said, then added, "but I'm sure she'll be only too happy to talk to Dr. Pierce. Hold on a moment, please."

Crumley's face registered mild surprise that a reverend mother would be "only too happy" to speak with a fire-breathing heathen, and then it registered complete surprise when that distinguished religious came on the line.

"*Ciao,* Hawkeye," she said. "How's my favorite heathen-cutter?"

"One moment, please, Reverend Mother," Hazel said, somewhat flustered. "I'll ring Hawkeye for you."

"Dr. Pierce," he said, coming on the line.

"Your dime, Hawkeye," Reverend Mother Superior Bernadette of Lourdes* said. "Start talking."

"Hi-ya, Bernie," Hawkeye said.

"How're things on the well-known rock-bound coast?" the Reverend Mother inquired. "Specifically, how's Esther and that back-sliding crony of yours?"

"Trapper John** sends regards," Hawkeye said. "And I'm calling about Esther."

"Nothing wrong, I hope."

"Not yet," Hawkeye said. "You know how Hot Lips† keeps asking Esther to come down there for a little vacation?"

"What about it?"

"Well, she's got reservations on the nine-fifteen plane tomorrow morning."

"Well, that's grand," the Reverend Mother said. "I'll look forward to seeing her."

"The reason she's going is so that she and Hot Lips

---

* Reverend Mother Superior Bernadette of Lourdes, M.D., F.A.C.S., Chief of Staff of the Gates of Heaven Hospital, New Orleans, Louisiana, and Dr. Pierce became both professionally and personally acquainted several years before when Dr. Pierce operated upon His Eminence John Patrick Mulcahy, Archbishop of Swengchan. The details of this ecumenical cutting have been recorded for posterity in *M*A*S*H Goes to New Orleans* (Pocket Books) for those wtih a prurient interest in surgical procedures.

** The reference here is to John Francis Xavier McIntyre, M.D., F.A.C.S., who in his college days was accused by a University of Maine coed of trapping her in the gentlemen's rest facility of a Boston & Maine railroad car. The accusation, which Dr. McIntyre denied vehemently, came after the pair was caught, more or less, *flagrante delicto*, by a nosy conductor. Despite Dr. McIntyre's denial, the accusation was generally believed; hence, the designation of "Trapper John."

† Dr. Pierce here referred to the Reverend Mother Emeritus Margaret H. W. Wilson, R.N., Chief of Nursing Education at the Ms. Prudence MacDonald Memorial School of Nursing of New Orleans, which was affiliated with Gates of Heaven Hospital. How Chief of Nursing Education Wilson, R.N., came to be known as "Hot Lips" is far too complicated a tale for a footnote. Those with a burning desire to know immediately are directed to the original *M*A*S*H* and all its sequels, which Pocket Books, as a public service, makes available on the racks of the better bus terminals and other such places. Those with a modicum of patience will find an explanation later in these pages.

can go to the Saints-Cowboys game," Hawkeye added, "in Dallas."

"Uh-oh," the Reverend Mother said.

"So what I was thinking, Bernie," Hawkeye said, "was that if you could get away . . . "

"I've got a hospital to run, you know," she said.

"All work and no play, Bernie," Hawkeye said, "as I was saying just the other day to Ben Franklin."

There was a pause, and then the Reverend Mother said, somewhat cheerfully, "You may have an idea, Hawkeye. I'd love to see the game. God knows, I haven't had a couple of days off in a long time. And His Eminence is going."

"Sauce for the goose . . . " Hawkeye said.

"I hadn't thought of it in quite those terms, Hawkeye," the Reverend Mother said. "But what about tickets?"

"You can have mine," Hawkeye said. "I really can't get away."

"That's very kind of you," the Reverend Mother said.

"Greater love hath no man than to lay down his Saints-Cowboys tickets for his operating-room nurse," Hawkeye said.

"Forgive me for sounding cynical, Hawkeye," the Reverend Mother said, "but getting me to go wouldn't have anything to do with what it said in the paper today, would it?"

"What did it say in the paper, Bernie?"

"It said that, as usual, Hot Lips would serve as drum majorette for the Bayou Perdu Council, K. of C., Marching Band."

"You don't like band music, Bernie?" Hawkeye asked.

"You know what I mean, Hawkeye," she said.

"What I was really worried about, Bernie," Hawkeye said, "was not so much the game, but the party after the game."

"I have no intention of going to the K. of C. party," she said. "You should know better!"

"That's the whole point," Hawkeye said. "Now that I'm exposed, if you don't go to the party, Esther Flanagan won't go to the party. That way I stand a much better chance of getting her back right away, instead of after thirty days on the Texas road gang for inciting to riot, or being drunk or disorderly, or worse."

"Okay, you got it," the Reverend Mother said. "With a little bit of luck, I'll be able to talk Hot Lips out of going, too."

"Bless you, Reverend Mother!" Hawkeye said piously.

At this point, the conversation was terminated. Mr. T. Alfred Crumley, Sr., had the distinct impression that the Reverend Mother had slammed her handset down in the cradle.

Chapter Two

"Politics," as one sagacious* observer of the political scene once observed, "makes strange bedfellows."**

This seemed especially true in the case of the three distinguished representatives of the people of New Jersey, Illinois and Texas who met that same day aboard a forty-eight-foot Bertram shrimpboat† dubbed

---

* "Sagacious," adjective (from the Latin *sagire*): acute in perception, especially by smell.

** He was making reference to the relationship between two or more politicians, and not to that strange bedfellow relationship that seems to exist between politicians and non-typing secretaries and other, generally female, government employees.

† Under the laws of the Great State of Texas, "workboats"—those used, for example, to harvest shrimp and oysters—are taxed at a much lower rate than pleasure boats or yachts. The owner of *The Ayes of Texas* religiously saw to it that once every six months one of the crew threw a shrimp net over the side for not less than an hour at a time. On one memorable occasion three years before, the net had actually hauled in three shrimp and a catfish. The owner had them stuffed by a taxidermist, who gave him a special "Congressional" rate, and they now hang in his office.

20

The Ayes of Texas as it sailed up the Potomac River near our nation's capital.

Outwardly, Congressmen Antonio J. "Tiny Tony" Bambino (Ethnic Democrat, N.J.), Vladimir "Vibrato Val" Vishnefsky (Polish Republican, Ill.) and Davy Crockett "Alamo" Jones (Liberal-Conservative, Tex.) had little in common, except their hair, which in all three cases was silver-gray and lovingly coiffed.

Tiny Tony Bambino, seated behind his desk, bore a carefully cultivated resemblance to the hatchet-featured, flowing-haired Roman senators one sees immortalized on tombs and other memorials around Rome (Italy). All of his official campaign photographs showed him seated behind his desk, a highly polished mahogany object nine feet long and five feet wide that had been a little gift to the congressman from the Sicilian-American Protective Society. The SAPS' leader had had a little difficulty with the Immigration and Naturalization Service, and they appreciated what Tiny Tony had done in his behalf, even if it had all been in vain, and the gentleman in question had been deported in chains.

It was only when the congressman stood up that one sort of noticed his size. Including his silver-gray, two-and-a-half-inch pompadour, the Vice-Chairman of the House Committee on Honesty in Government stood five-feet two-inches tall. The visual result of his massive, Roman, leonine head and broad shoulders on his short frame was to suggest that he had been assembled from mismatching display-dummy parts by a window dresser who had been at the sauce.

Congressman Vibrato Val Vishnefsky, on the other hand, came with a six-foot, five-inch body. He had what he thought of as a Lincolnesque Adam's apple, and from that area downward his body seemed to taper to a point. Soaking wet, Vibrato Val weighed one hundred fifty pounds. His silver-gray locks were almost shoulder length and completely hid his ears. One of his detractors (and there were, frankly, many of these) once compared him to a dripping vanilla ice-cream cone.

The congressman was one of the Hill's most accomplished orators. When it was known that Vibrato Val was to make another of his impassioned speeches to the Congress,* everybody not otherwise engaged came to the floor. It was really something to see his Adam's apple vibrate like that.

Like Tiny Tony Bambino, Vibrato Val had spent many years in the Congress, rising, via seniority, like a bubble of swamp gas, to the upper echelons of congressional leadership—specifically to become the Vice-Chairman of the House Committee on Closing Tax Loopholes and Soaking the Rich.

Their host, *el capitán* of *The Ayes of Texas,* the Honorable Davy Crockett Jones, was, it must be admitted, the most handsome of the three. He stood six-feet-two, had broad shoulders, trim hips, white teeth and blue eyes. He had a firm grip, a firm jaw and a firm handshake.

As his publicity handouts repeatedly reminded one and all, Davy "Alamo" Jones had been a star football player, a forward, while at the University of Texas, until a back injury had forced him off the team.

He had hurt his back not, as legend had it, in his very first varsity game, but in what might well be called his very first scrimmage of life, specifically in the back seat of a 1952 Ford convertible parked at the time behind the Tau Omega sorority house.

The convertible belonged to one Ida-Sue Dal-

* The congressman was flatly opposed to sin, war and wasteful governmental spending, and foursquare in favor of God, Mother, Country and the Congressional Pension System.

rymple, a tall and statuesque Tau Omega senior who had spent three years so far at the University of Texas looking without success for someone suitable on whom she could bestow what she thought of at the time as her pearl of great price, and with whom she could subsequently march hand in hand down the rocky road of life.

The moment Ida-Sue saw Davy Crockett Jones (she was a pom-pom girl with the university's marching band; the first time she saw him was when he, together with his teammates, ran onto the field to the strains of "The Eyes of Texas") she knew that her search was over. Here was the handsome man she had been waiting for.

By the time the game was over, she had learned all that she felt she needed to know about him. Most important, he was unmarried. Four hours after she first laid eyes on him, Ida-Sue Dalrymple found herself lying under him in the back seat of the convertible her adoring father had given her for her last birthday.

Davy Crockett Jones had moaned, and despite her relative inexperience in situations of that sort, Ida-Sue knew immediately that it was not a groan of either passion or ecstasy.

"Darlin'," she said, "what's the matter?"

"I hurt my back," Davy Crockett Jones said, "something awful."

There was a moment's thoughtful silence, and then Ida-Sue responded.

"Great!" she said.

"Pardon me, Betty-Sue?" Davy Crockett Jones said.

"It's *Ida*-Sue, darlin'," Ida-Sue gently corrected him. "You're going to have to remember that. It seems the very least you can do, now that you've stolen my pearl of great price."

"Girl, whatever is you talking about?" Davy Crockett Jones replied. "I never seen no pearl."

"Never mind, darlin'," Ida-Sue said. "The important thing is that we now have a good excuse to get you off the football team before someone smashes your darlin' nose flat with his knee, or something."

"You sure talk funny, Betty-Sue," Davy Crockett Jones replied.

"For the last time, darlin', that's *Ida*-Sue," she replied. "Now, get off me so's we can go into the sorority house and announce our engagement."

"Our what?"

"Our engagement, darlin'," she said. "I accept."

"Excuse me, but I don't remember proposing."

"But you did, darlin'," she replied. "I remember it perfectly."

"I can't afford no wife," Davy Crockett Jones replied. "I'm here on a football scholarship. And you didn't say nothing about getting married when you brought me out here. All you asked was if I wanted to fool around some."

"You're never going to have to worry about money again, darlin'," Ida-Sue replied. "Daddy's got lots of money, and Uncle Hiram's got even more."

"No foolin'?"

"No fooling, darlin'," Ida-Sue said.

Davy Crockett Jones rolled off her. Ida-Sue Dalrymple looked up at his massive chest, his flat stomach, his white teeth and his darlin' nose.

"On second thought," Ida-Sue Dalrymple said, "I think it would be better if we eloped."

"You mean right now?" Davy Crockett Jones replied.

"Davy, darlin'," Ida-Sue responded, "you've swept me right off my feet, that's what you've done!"

They were married that very night (actually at

three-thirty the next morning) by a justice of the peace in Lubbock.

Nine months later Mrs. Davy Crockett Jones was delivered of a daughter, their first and only child.

When the proud father (by then a junior at the university, with a part-time job as Executive Vice-President of Dalrymple Oil & Gas, Inc.) looked down at his wife and infant daughter, his bride looked back up at him through misty eyes and said, "I can see it now, darlin', you in a morning coat, with a carnation in your lapel, walking through the Rose Garden with little Scarlett on your arm while the U.S. Marine Corps Band plays 'I Love You Truly, Dear.'"

"They still got you pretty well doped up, huh, Ida-Sue?" Davy Crockett Jones asked. "You ain't making much sense."

"I've asked you, darlin', not to say 'ain't.' What would people think if you said 'ain't' when you were President of the United States?"

"I don't want to be President of the United States," Davy Crockett Jones replied. "All I want is a little spread of my own by the side of the road where I can be a friend of man."

"Let me put it to you this way, darlin'," Ida-Sue said, shifting baby Scarlett from one side to the other. "If you really don't want your loving wife and mother of your child to be the First Lady of the United States, that's perfectly all right. I'll just go back to Daddy on the ranch, and you can just go back to kicking dirt clods."

"Whatever you say, Ida-Sue," Davy Crockett Jones replied. "You know that all I want in this world is to make you happy."

"*I* know, darlin'," Ida-Sue Dalrymple Jones replied. "*You're* the one who keeps forgettin'."

Davy Crockett Jones was graduated from the Uni-

versity of Texas the following year (Bachelor of Arts,
football science) and almost immediately left with his
family for England. This is the period of his life described in his official biographical literature as that
during which he "studied economics and diplomacy in
Europe."

The Crocketts spent three years in London. It took
that long (painful experiments with a series of speech
teachers having been a conspicuous failure) to rid the
future congressman of his west Texas drawl and to
cure him, once and for all, of saying "ain't." The economics he studied were, in truth, limited to calculating
the odds at a game of chance called *vingt-et-un**
which he played at length (and with some success) at
the better London gambling establishments.

Through her connections with England-Irish &
Texas Petroleum, Ltd., a subsidiary of Dalrymple Oil
& Gas, Mrs. Jones was able to introduce her husband
to some of the most exalted of British High Society.
He even got to ride to the hounds.**

Their European sojourn came to an end when
Lothario Dalrymple, Chairman of the Board of Dalrymple Petroleum, and Ida-Sue's beloved Daddy, was
called to that Great Board Meeting in the Sky.

Shortly after the funeral, the will was read. Ida-Sue
Dalrymple Jones was surprised to learn that her
Daddy had not, as she believed (and, indeed, as
Daddy himself had told her), owned all the stock of

---

* *Ving-et-un*, a game played with cards, is similar in many ways to
blackjack, a game in which, pre-football scholarship, Mr. Jones had
whiled away many an idle hour at the Last Gas for Ninety Miles service
station, restaurant and pool hall in his native Snake Rock, Texas.

** To this day, in fact, The Upper Baldwyn-upon-Thistle Hunt always
has a merry chuckle recalling the congressman's first ride to the hounds
with them. It was the first time that the hunt had ever seen the fox
pursued by a rider in a ten-gallon hat, singing "Getalong Little Doggie"
at the top of his lungs, and ultimately lassoing, throwing and tying the
fox with a lariat.

the corporation. His brother, Hiram, in fact, owned almost half, specifically, forty-nine percent of it. Ten percent of the stock, moreover, of the stock of which her Daddy, in legal terms, had "died possessed," was left in a bequest to Miss Francine Schwartz, her father's personal secretary for many years. That left but forty-one percent of the stock for Lothario to leave to his "beloved baby daughter," as the will put it.

This was some ten percent shy of a majority, but Ida-Sue Dalrymple Jones, like her father before her, was not one to permit her well-laid plans to be shoved aside by a minor technicality. The odds against Uncle Hiram, who had not left his ranch for thirty-five years —not even to plant his only brother—challenging her take-over of the company were negligible.

The stockholders (which is really to say Ida-Sue, attempts to locate Miss Schwartz having been futile) elected Davy Crockett Jones, who had been Executive Vice-President all along, to be President and Chairman of the Board. A faithful underling was entrusted with the actual operation of the company, and Ida-Sue was now free to begin the next step of her plan to go down in the history books as the first Texas Lady to be First Lady of the Republic.

The future congressman went down to an ignoble defeat in his first bid for elected office. He ran on what seemed at the time to Ida-Sue to be a sure thing, voting his native Snake Rock County wet. Still something of a political novice, Ida Sue was unaware of a political reality, that on a question vis-à-vis the legal sale of booze, the combined efforts of hard-shell Baptists and bootleggers to keep an area dry are unassailable.

The following year, however, Davy Crockett Jones entered and won election to the Texas State Legislature as the Temperance Party's candidate from Snake Rock County. By then Ida-Sue had learned well her

basic principles of practical politics. She went first to
Big Sam Kegley, the generally acknowledged dean of
Snake Rock County's bootleggers, and told him that
not only had she seen the error of her ways, but that
she was willing to make up for it. For every dollar
that Big Sam saw fit to contribute to her husband's
campaign, she would personally provide a matching
dollar. She would, moreover, see to it that Big Sam's
name was kept out of the papers.*

Big Sam put up twenty-five thousand dollars. Ida-
Sue, true to her word, put up a matching twenty-five
thousand dollars and donated the whole to the Snake
Rock County Baptist Battle Against Booze. After only
pro forma objections, the Internal Revenue Service
accepted her claim that the fifty thousand dollars was
a religious contribution, and, as such, deductible.

Davy Crockett Jones served four terms in the state
legislature, and then, in Ida-Sue's judgment, it was
time for him to go after the big time. He announced
his candidacy on the Liberal ticket to go for the seat
of Congressman John David "Brother Dave" Murgatroyd, a Conservative who had represented his district
in Congress for twenty-six years.

Alamo Jones' campaign had really not been doing
too well, actually, until the Dallas Police Department's
vice squad, in response to what they later termed
"information from a public-spirited anonymous in-
former," raided the Bali Hai Motel and discovered
Brother Dave Murgatroyd frolicking in his birthday
suit with three teen-aged Mexican-American hookers.

Normally, of course, in Texas, as elsewhere, the
police who had burst through the door of the Bali Hai
Motel room would have been perfectly willing to ac-

* The Snake Rock County *Intelligencer & Tribune,* a weekly newspaper, was the only newspaper in Snake Rock County. It was a subsidiary of Dalrymple Oil & Gas.

cept whatever explanation the congressman offered
for being where he was and doing what he was doing.
But by a strange coincidence, "Eagle Eye" Mac-
Namara, ace photo-journalist of the Snake Rock
County *Intelligencer & Tribune,* just happened to be
in the vice squad room of the Dallas police station
when the telephoned tip vis-à-vis the hanky-panky going on in Room 117 of the Bali Hai came in. He ac-
companied the vice squad on their appointed rounds
and was thus able to take the widely circulated photograph of the congressman wearing nothing but two
naked Mexican-American young ladies and a look of
surprise and indignation.

Thus ended the long and distinguished career of the
Honorable Brother Dave Murgatroyd; there was nothing left for him but to become a registered lobbyist,
after, of course, the traditional "Bon Voyage" junket
around the world at public expense ritually awarded
to congressmen who are either defeated at the polls,
or who, as in the case of Congressman Murgatroyd,
announce they will not stand for reelection for reasons
of health.

Davy Crockett "Alamo" Jones not only ran uncon-
tested for the seat Brother Dave was vacating, but
with the endorsement of both the Liberal and Conservative parties. He prevailed upon Eagle Eye Mac-
Namara to abandon his promising journalistic career
to enter the field of public service as his Executive Director of Media Relations, a position Mr. MacNamara
holds to this day, and for which the grateful taxpayers
compensate him at $38,570 per annum.

Congressman Jones experienced very little trouble
making the transition from Texas state legislator to
United States Congressman. For one thing, he hired,
intact, the entire staff of dedicated public servants who
had for so long served Brother Dave Murgatroyd.

These people not only told him what to vote for, and what to vote against, thus relieving him of the onerous chore of deciding for himself, but they were able to advise him which of the more powerful members of the House might be susceptible to taking a flier in oil exploration, and who would, should the flier be financially successful, be most grateful.

This frankly proved to be a more expensive means of attracting favorable attention of his seniors than, say, expressing wonder at the beauty of their grandchildren, letting them win at golf or even flying them down to the ranch in a Dalrymple Oil & Gas airplane for "a little Texas hospitality."

But as Ida-Sue confessed in the privacy of their boudoir in the little penthouse atop the Park-Sheraton Hotel, "No sacrifice was too great when it came to climbing up the ladder to the White House."

The way the plan worked was this: Dalrymple Oil & Gas' Exploration Division would, after due investigation of seismographic charts and other little tricks of the trade, conclude that the odds were very good that oil would be found at, say, 18,500 feet beneath the west Texas sagebrush. Dalrymple Oil & Gas would then install a "rig" and "make a hole" to 18,250 feet. At that point, they would become discouraged and "abandon" the hole. All the money spent to drill the hole to 18,250 feet would be recorded in their books in red ink as a loss.

That amount could then be deducted from income for tax purposes.

Ida-Sue and Alamo would then form another company, say, for example, The West Texas-Hohokus, New Jersey, Oil Company and sell shares in it to, for example, the Honorable Tiny Tony Bambino of Hohokus, New Jersey. Then the West Texas-Hohokus, New Jersey, Oil Company would buy the mineral rights to the land on which Dalrymple Oil had dug the "dry" 18,250-foot hole.

A somewhat smaller, and thus more inexpensive, drilling rig, called a "work-over rig," would then be placed over the abandoned hole, and the hole would be extended another 250 feet.

"Eureka! Oil!" the cry would go up, and the royalties would begin to flow in. Congressman Bambino's faith in the oil industry in general, and in the all-around wisdom of his new companion in the halls of Congress, the Honorable Alamo Jones, would be rewarded. Not only were his profits from his investment regarded as a capital gain, but there was the oil depletion allowance, which rather effectively cut into the share the government would normally get as taxes.

To keep the whole thing honest, of course, Congressman Bambino and Congressman Vibrato Val Vishnefsky actually did put up some real money: fifteen hundred dollars in the case of Congressman Bambino, and two thousand dollars in the case of Congressman Vishenfsky, which latter sum saw Vishnefsky become sole owner of the Midland, Texas, & Cicero, Illinois, Oil Company.

The best-laid plans of mice, men and ambitious congressmen's wives, however, as the saying goes, sometimes go astray. And this was the reason Congressman Bambino and Congressman Vishnefsky had decided to have a little *tête-à-tête* with Congressman Alamo Jones aboard *The Ayes of Texas,* cruising far from prying eyes midstream in the Potomac River.

What had gone wrong was that when the work-over rigs of the West Texas-Hohokus, New Jersey, Oil Company and the Midland, Texas, & Cicero, Illinois, Oil Company had drilled down another couple of hundred feet, and then another couple of hundred feet and finally a total of about another one thousand feet, all the drill bits had encountered was more rocky sand.

Chapter Three

When Vibrato Val had telephoned Alamo and let it be known that he and Tiny Tony wished to confer with him in confidence and at the earliest possible moment about a matter of some importance to them all, Alamo suspected that it had little or nothing to do with the nation's business.

If it had something to do with the nation's business, he cleverly concluded, he would have been summoned to either Vibrato Val's or Tiny Tony's office right there on Capitol Hill. Neither Vibrato Val nor Tiny Tony would have felt it necessary, as they did now, to meet with him aboard *The Ayes of Texas* for a midnight cruise up the Potomac in a rain storm.

Although he, of course, immediately responded with what he hoped sounded like enthusiasm to Vibrato Val's little suggestion, the truth of the matter was that attending the annual reunion of Former University of Texas Marching Band Pom-Pom Girls, the high point

of the Texas social calendar, which was being held
this year at the Shamrock Hotel in Houston, did not
strike him as particularly thrilling.

Ida-Sue, as Alamo thought of it, had sort of a flair
for dealing with Vibrato Val and Tiny Tony that he
just didn't have. They seemed to more or less understand each other, despite the vast difference in language.

But there was nothing to be done. As Ida-Sue herself was always saying, Alamo reminded himself,
"You're a congressman now, dummy, so try to stop
kicking clods." Certainly, Alamo reasoned, there was
no reason he shouldn't meet with two other congressmen for what Vibrato Val had described as a little
chat.

Ida-Sue had taken Eagle Eye MacNamara, Alamo's Executive Director of Media Relations, with
her to make sure that her speech to the assembled former pom-pom girls received wide coverage in the
Texas press. That worried Alamo at first, until he concluded that since the meeting was going to be confiden-
tial, he probably wouldn't need Eagle Eye's services.

Alamo was waiting at the rail of *The Ayes of Texas*
when the small power boat splashed through the fog
and rain and pulled alongside. He had put on his cap-
tain's hat for the occasion, and his blue blazer with the
brass buttons and the white flannel trousers.

"Welcome aboard, mates!" Alamo said as Vibrato
Val and Tiny Tony climbed up the stairs (or "ladder,"
as it is known in yachting circles).

Neither Vibrato Val nor Tiny Tony responded to
his greeting, save for a "follow me" motion of his hand
on the part of Tiny Tony. They led Alamo Jones to
the main cabin of *The Ayes of Texas* and took seats at
the mess table, above which hung nearly identical oil

portraits of two scantily dressed young women waving pom-poms.

"You're not too bright, Jones, you know that?" Tiny Tony said. "With what's been going on lately, hanging up pictures of two bimbos isn't what you could call smart."

"Tony . . . I can call you Tony, can't I?" Alamo began.

"Congressman Bambino to you, Tex," Tiny Tony said.

"Those are portraits of my wife and our little Scarlett," Alamo said.

"You're kidding!" Tiny Tony said.

"I wouldn't kid you, Congressman," Alamo said. "Perish the thought!"

"Huh," Tiny Tony snorted.

"Well, gentlemen," Vibrato Val boomed, "shall we get down to business?"

"Good idea, Val," Alamo said.

"That's Congressman Vishnefsky to you, Tex," Tiny Tony said. "You're a newcomer around here."

"No disrespect intended, sir."

"Watch it in the future," Tiny Tony said.

"How may I help you gentlemen?" Alamo asked.

"Let me put it to you this way, son," Vibrato Val said sonorously. "You're something of a disappointment to us both."

"I'm very sorry to hear that," Alamo said.

"We saw a future for you, Tex," Tiny Tony said, "a brilliant future."

"You really could have been somebody around the Hill," Vibrato Val added.

"We thought you were our kind of people," Tiny Tony said.

"I was even thinking of putting you up for membership in the Congressional Breakfast Prayer Meeting Club, Incorporated,"* Vibrato Val said.

"I would have liked that," Alamo said.

"And then this!" Tiny Tony said.

"And then what, sir?"

"It's a good thing for you, Tex, that you're a member of Congress. Otherwise, I'm afraid I'd have to think of you as nothing more than a lousy con man," Tiny Tony said.

"I don't quite follow you, sir," Alamo said.

"We trusted you, Tex," Vibrato Val said. "We even gave you money, didn't we, Tony?"

"I personally gave you fifteen hundred dollars," Tiny Tony said, "my entire refund for my March unused stationery allowance."

"But that was an investment!" Alamo responded, having finally gotten a rough idea of what was being discussed.

"An investment? You make money from investments, not lose it!" Vibrato Val said.

"Sometimes, Congressmen," Alamo said, "you lose money when you make an investment." He had heard that in Europe.

"Civilians might make investments that lose money," Tiny Tony said, "but not congressmen."

"You led us to believe it was a sure thing, Jones," Vibrato Val said. "It's not nice to lie to your betters."

"These things happen all the time," Alamo tried to

---

* The Congressional Breakfast Prayer Meeting Club, Incorporated, owns and operates facilities (including a steam and sauna room, a massage parlor, restaurant and what is euphemistically described as a "lounge") on Northwest K Street. Although the club is open twenty-four hours a day, breakfast is not served. Nor, with the exception of the Diety being asked to grant special favor vis-à-vis the outcome of dice or the next card to be dealt, are prayers often heard. Membership in the club, however, does permit congressional receptionists to inform constitutents that the congressman they seek, whose hangover precludes his presence on the Hill or upon whom Lady Luck is smiling at the poker table, is "at the Breakfast Prayer Meeting."

explain. "You don't always find oil when you sink a hole."

"Don't try to confuse the issue, son, with a bunch of extraneous details," Vibrato Val said. "You're dealing with a couple of experts in confusing the issues. You just stick to the facts. And the facts are that we put money in your oil deal because we trusted you, and what happened?"

Alamo opened his mouth to speak, but Tiny Tony beat him to it.

"I had a call from Texas this morning, that's what happened," Tiny Tony said. "And you know what I heard, Tex?"

"No, sir."

"I heard that my oil well was a dry hole—that's what I heard. Now, how could something like that happen, Tex?"

"Well, that's probably because there's no oil down there," Alamo said.

"Do I look like a dummy, Jones?" Tiny Tony asked. "The kind of a congressman who'd give you his entire March stationery refund to drill a dry hole?"

"No, sir," Alamo said firmly.

"And you know what I got in the mail today, son?" Vibrato Val said, sadness in every syllable.

"No, sir, I don't," Alamo confessed.

"I got a little bag of sand—that's what I got. A little bag of sand. It wasn't even a full bag of sand. And it had a tag on it. You know what that tag said, son?"

"No, sir."

"It said, 'Well Sample, Midland & Cicero Well Number One, Twenty-Thousand Feet'—that's what it said. Do you know what that means, son?"

"Yes, sir," Alamo said brightly. "That means they took a sample of what the drill bit was running into at twenty thousand feet."

"What it means, son," Vibrato Val corrected him, "is that Vladimir Vishnefsky, out of the goodness of his heart, put two thousand dollars of his hard-earned money into your stupid hole in the ground—that's what it means."

"Gentlemen," Alamo said, "I understand exactly how you feel. But put your minds at rest. I'll have certified checks refunding every nickel delivered by messenger just as soon as the banks open in the morning."

"Like hell you will!" Vibrato Val said. "You sold me an oil well, and I want an oil well—one with oil in it."

"What kind of dummies do you take us for?" Tiny Tony said.

"Let me put it to you this way, son," Vibrato Val said. "Just ask yourself this question: What kind of a career is a none-too-bright clod-kicker going to have in Congress once the word gets around that he's been selling dry oil wells to every senior member?"

"Taking advantage of their trust in him as a fellow solon?" Tiny Tony added. "Promising his fellow statesmen an oil well and delivering a lousy little bag of sand?"

"It's not as if you were fleecing the public, son," Vibrato Val said. "We all do that. But even someone as dumb as you should know that fleecing a fellow congressman is a no-no."

"I'll tell you what I'll do," Alamo Jones said. "To straighten out this unfortunate misunderstanding . . . "

"There's no misunderstanding, son," Vibrato Val said. "We understand perfectly."

"What I was going to suggest, sirs," Alamo said, "is that you sell me your oil wells. I'll pay you whatever you think they're worth, and you'll have a check just as soon as the banks open in the morning."

"What do you take us for, Tex, a couple of crooks?" Vibrato Val asked.

"You didn't really think that Congressman Vishnefsky and I would actually take good money for a worthless oil well, did you?" Tiny Tony asked.

"Of *course* not," Alamo Jones said firmly. Then he added, "But if you don't want money, what do you want?"

"Only what you promised, son," Vibrato Val Vishnefsky said, "an oil well."

"With oil in it," Tiny Tony added.

"One that we can see with our own eyes," Vibrato Val said. "Everything has to be on the up-and-up."

"How am I supposed to arrange for that? Alamo asked.

"You'll think of something, son," Vibrato Val said.

"Just let us know when—at your convenience, just so long as it's within the next two weeks—we can go look at our oil wells."

"More specifically, son," Vibrato Val added kindly, "at the oil coming out of our oil wells."

Alamo Jones knew there was only one thing to do: bring the problem to Ida-Sue. He would have gone ashore with Vibrato Val and Tiny Tony, but they said they didn't want to run the risk of anyone seeing them in the same boat with him, so he had to wait until the motorboat put them ashore and then returned for him.

But just as soon as he was able to reach the Park-Sheraton penthouse, he called Ida-Sue at the Shamrock in Houston.

"Where the hell have you been?" Ida-Sue greeted him. "I've been trying to get you for hours."

"We've got a little problem, Ida-Sue," Alamo said.

"My God, is it all over Washington already?"

"Is what all over Washington already?"

"What Scarlett has done to shame and humiliate me

before my friends," Ida-Sue said. "Before all of Texas! Before the world!"

"I don't quite follow you, Ida-Sue," Alamo said.

"I thought you said it was all over Washington."—

"You said that, darling," Alamo replied.

"Don't argue with me, Alamo," Ida-Sue said. "You know how upset I get when you argue with me."

"Sorry, darling," Alamo said. "You were telling me about Scarlett. What's Daddy Davy's little girl been up to now?"

"Daddy Davy's little girl just shamed and humiliated her mother—that'a what she did!" Ida-Sue said.

"Well, darling," Alamo said soothingly, "girls will be girls, you know."

"Shut up, dummy," Ida-Sue said, "before you really make me angry."

"Like I was saying, Ida-Sue," Alamo went on, "we have a little problem."

"I don't know what your problem is, Alamo," she replied, "but you can take my word for it, it's nothing compared to my problem."

"You haven't even heard what mine is," Alamo replied.

"Don't argue with me, you clod-kicker!" Ida-Sue replied rather excitedly.

"What exactly is *your* problem, Ida-Sue, honey?"

"I can never hold my head up in the presence of any member of the F U T M B P P G again."

"Ida-Sue, honey, what's the F U T M B P P G? It seems to have slipped my mind."

"Former University of Texas Marching Band Pom-Pom Girls, dummy. I've told you that and told you that!"

"And what did little Scarlett do to embarrass you, Ida-Sue?"

"The *crème de la crème* of the annual F U T M B

P P G reunion is the mother-daughter banquet, Alamo.
You know that. The only people who get to sit at the
head table are F U T M B P P G mothers whose
daughters are now U T M B P P G's themselves."

"I know," Alamo replied.

"I've been looking forward to this since Scarlett was
born," Ida-Sue said.

"I know," Alamo said.

"You won't believe what that ungrateful daughter
of yours has done to me, Alamo," Ida-Sue said.

"What did she do, Ida-Sue?"

"She was supposed to meet me here at the Shamrock at nine o'clock this morning," Ida-Sue said.

"I thought the banquet was set for tonight, Ida-
Sue."

"It is. We were supposed to spend the day rehearsing."

"Rehearsing? Rehearsing what? How to eat? What
is it, a Japanese banquet with chopsticks?"

"You're really dumb, Alamo, you know that?" Ida-
Sue replied. "Dear old Daddy was right about you. He
said you were the dumbest man he'd ever met."

"That's not very kind of you, Ida-Sue," Alamo said.
"But we digress. What exactly were you supposed to
rehearse all day, I mean, since it wasn't how to eat
with chopsticks?"

"Texas, Texas, rah-rah-rah, of course," Ida-Sue
said. "What else?"

"You want to go over that again, Ida-Sue?"

"Texas, Texas, rah-rah-rah," she obligingly repeated.

"Texas, Texas, rah-rah-rah," Alamo said. "Of
course. I should have known right off. Exactly what
does that mean, Ida-Sue?"

"We were supposed to do it together," Ida-Sue explained. "Scarlett was going to do the back flips on the

Texas, Texas, and I was going to shake the pom-poms on the rah-rah-rah."

"I see."

"But I was going to really surprise them," Ida-Sue said. "I've been practicing myself. And instead of me just standing there shaking the pom-poms while Scarlett was doing the backflips, I was going to do the backflips right along with her. I'm in much better shape than any of the other F U T M B P P G mommies, and when you've got it, flaunt it, as Daddy always used to say."

"Sure you are," Alamo replied. "So what happened?"

"You wouldn't believe it if I told you," Ida-Sue said. "I've never been so humiliated in my life."

"You split your cheerleader's pants doing the backflips?" Alamo inquired after a moment's thought.

"That's another thing wrong about you, Alamo," Ida-Sue said. "All you think about is S.E.X."

"That's not true, Ida-Sue, and you know it," Alamo said.

"And come to think of it, all you *do* is think about it, which is even worse," Ida-Sue went on. "But it was even worse than that."

"What could be worse than splitting your pants doing backflips at the F U T M B P P G annual reunion?"

"Having your daughter humiliate you by rejecting all that you hold dear—that's what," Ida-Sue said, a suggestion of triumph mixed with her tone of pain.

"How did she do that?" Alamo asked.

"She didn't show up, that's how she did it," Ida-Sue replied.

"Well, you know how girls are," Scarlett's father said. "Maybe something came up. Maybe Mr. Right came along, for example."

"I'll tell you what happened," Ida-Sue said. "I sent

Eagle Eye MacNamara with the limousine to get her at school, and she wasn't there."

"Didn't she leave a note or something?"

"I'll say she did. I'll read the note," Ida-Sue said.

"Go ahead," Alamo said.

" 'Dear Momma,' it says," Ida-Sue said, " 'I have come to the conclusion that there must be more to life than shaking pom-poms and doing backflips, and so I have gone off on my own to find a new life helping my fellowman in some small way.' "

"Gee," Alamo replied, "that really brings a lump to your throat, doesn't it?"

"Alamo," Ida-Sue said, menace in every syllable, "Scarlett had no right, no right at all, to go off on her own to help her fellowman in some small way when her own mother needed her for Texas, Texas, rah-rah-rah at the F U T M B P P G annual reunion, and you know it."

"You're right, of course, Ida-Sue. You always are."

"I know I am. Now, I want you to find her, Alamo, and have a good talk with her."

"How am I going to find her?"

"You're a congressman, dummy. You keep forgetting that. Send the F.B.I. looking for her."

"Speaking of Congress, Ida-Sue," Alamo said.

"What about it?" she asked.

"We have a little problem, Ida-Sue," Alamo said. "That's what I called about."

"Let's have it," she said.

"I just had a little talk with Vibrato Val Vishnefsky and Tiny Tony Bambino."

"So what?"

"They're a little unhappy about their dry holes, Ida-Sue. They say I promised them oil wells, and they want them."

"God, Alamo, you're really stupid. Just tell them

the wells came in and send each one a check. Even you should have been able to figure that out by yourself."

"Well, someone in the drilling department sent them reports saying the holes were dry. They don't want the money; they want a flowing well. Vibrato Val says everything has to be on the up and up."

There was a pause.

"The only place I know where there's oil for sure is on Uncle Hiram's spread," Ida-Sue replied. "I guess we'll just have to sink a couple of wells there."

"But we don't own Uncle Hiram's spread."

"I'll go down there myself." Ida-Sue replied, "and tell Uncle Hiram that Scarlett's future happiness absolutely depends on him letting us have 140 acres of his spread . . . God knows, he has enough . . . so we can put down a couple of wells."

"What's it got to do with Scarlett?"

"If Tiny Tony and Vibrato Val don't get their flowing wells, dummy, you're through in Congress. And if you're through in Congress, how are you going to be able to send the F.B.I. to find Scarlett?"

"Gee, Ida-Sue, you really know how to figure things out, don't you?" Alamo said respectfully.

"You get the F.B.I. started, and I'll fly down to Uncle Hiram's ranch," Ida-Sue replied. "There's no point in staying here, anyway. How can I be a F U T M B P P G Mommy now that Scarlett's run away?"

Chapter Four

The discerning reader may have noticed that co-mingled with Dr. Benjamin Franklin Pierce's generous tender of his tickets to the New Orleans Saints-Dallas Cowboys football game was a suggestion, however subtle, that the post-game social ritually sponsored by the Bayou Perdu Council, Knights of Columbus, might tend to become just a shade rowdy.

While it is, of course, true that chiefs of surgery, as a class, tend to be not only cynical and pessimistic, but first-class party-poopers, as well, it must be said that in this instance Dr. Pierce's concern was based on long and somewhat painful experience with the Bayou Perdu Council, K. of C., and was not simply a manifestation of the acid indigestion brought on by taking luncheon in the Spruce Harbor Medical Center staff cafeteria.

The fact that Dr. Pierce, a Protestant (of somewhat murky standing, to be sure, but a Protestant), is carried on the official rolls of the Bayou Perdu Council, K. of C., as Grand Exalted Surgeon and Healer and Social Disease Control Officer, when in other K. of C. organizations such high-level positions are granted only to those of the Catholic persuasion, is only the exposed tip of what might well be described as the iceberg of the Bayou Perdu Council differences from ordinary K. of C. councils.

Dr. Pierce was proposed for membership and appointment to his position by Col.* Jean-Pierre de la Chevaux, Knight Guardian of the Golden Fleece of the Bayou Perdu Council. As the succinct little phrase has it around Bayou Perdu, "What Horsey de la Chevaux wants, Horsey gets." Not only is Colonel de la Chevaux, as President, Chairman of the Board and Chief Executive Officer of the Chevaux Petroleum Corporation, International, the "boss" of 98.7 percent of the members of the Bayou Perdu Council, but lifetime holder of the Bayou Perdu Golden Fists, Boots and Ax-Handles Belt, awarded for excellence in what, around Bayou Perdu, are considered the manly arts.

Moreover, long before any members of the Bayou Perdu Council had laid eyes on Dr. Pierce, they had frequently heard from Horsey de la Chevaux how Dr. Pierce (and others) had saved his life and his leg when Horsey de la Chevaux had been a grievously wounded sergeant of the 223rd Infantry in Korea, and Dr. Pierce had been chief of surgery of the 4077th Mobile Army Surgical Hospital, or MASH.**

Dr. Pierce was, according to the minutes of that meeting, received into membership and elected to his

* Louisiana National Guard, retired.

** The details of Sergeant de la Chevaux's miltiary service, how he fell on the field of battle and how he was restored to good health, have been recorded in *M*A*S*H Goes to New Orleans* (Pocket Books), which is generally to be found on sale, a rose rising from the swamp, on most paperback bookracks.

office "by acclamation." Those same minutes also record for posterity that John Francis Xavier McIntyre,
M.D., F.A.C.S., was similarly enlisted and elected
(to be Deputy Grand Exalted Surgeon and Healer and
Social Disease Control Officer), and that, with certain
restrictions, the Bayou Perdu Council finally gave in
to pointed suggestions (from, among other people, the
Archbishop of New Orleans) that they authorize a
Ladies' Auxiliary.

"Any female of good reputation," the authorization
went, "is entitled to apply for membership in the Ladies' Auxiliary of the Bayou Perdu Council, K. of C.,
provided only that such applicants be retired officers,
in the grade of lieutenant colonel or better, of the U.S.
Army Nurse Corps." By a strange coincidence, only
one female, Margaret Houlihan Wachauf Wilson,
R.N., met those criteria. Nurse Wilson, or "Hot Lips,"
as she was known to her comrades-in-arms of the
4077th MASH, became the first, and for a long time,
only, member of the Bayou Perdu Council, K. of C.,
Ladies' Auxiliary.*

The love affair (often one-sided) between the Bayou
Perdu Council, K. of C., and the New Orleans Saints
football team goes back beyond the recruitment of
Doctors Pierce and McIntyre and Nurses Wilson and
Flanagan. It goes back, in fact, and to use the quaint
patois of the bayou country, to Before Horsey's Gas, or
B.H.G. B.H.G. obviously requires explanation.

Five years after Technical Sergeant Jean-Pierre de
la Chevaux, late of the 223rd Infantry, was medically
retired from the U.S. Army on a fifty percent disability

---

* Two years ago, again at Colonel de la Chevaux's suggestion, the
membership criteria were relaxed somewhat by the addition of the
words "or in the grade of lieutenant commander, or better, or the Navy
Nurse Corps." Shortly afterward, Esther Flanagan, Lieutenant Commander, U.S. Navy Nurse Corps, retired, became the second member
of the Ladies' Auxiliary.

pension for his wounds, the state of Louisiana, wishing
to take advantage of some $295 million that happened
to be lying around unspent in the federal highway fund,
announced that it was going to build a super highway
from the Texas border to the Mississippi border.

Everything went swimmingly until it was discovered
that someone actually owned sixteen thousand acres
of land in the vicinity of Bayou Perdu, through which
the superslab was to run. It was hard to believe at first
(the property was described, accurately, as "swamp,
with quicksand, brackish water and utterly unfit for
any conceivable use by man or beast"), but a search of
the records proved conclusively that His Most Catholic Majesty, Louis XIV, had, indeed, affixed the royal
signature to a land grant for one Jean-Phillipe, Sieur
de la Chevaux, awarding him eight thousand hectares
of His Most Catholic Majesty's land in the province
of Louisiana.*

Inquiries made of the Chancellory of the Archdiocese of New Orleans revealed that descendants of the
Sieur de la Chevaux had lived continually on the
property since the time of the land grant, and that the
present owner was a retired army sergeant named
Jean-Pierre de la Chevaux.

Initial attempts to meet with Horsey to discuss putting a highway across his swamp met with failure. The
highway department engineers were mistaken by
Horsey and his friends for representatives of the State

---

* Scholars are generally agreed that King Louis suspected the Sieur
de la Chevaux of fooling around with the Queen, and that His Majesty
was fully aware that the land he was granting was worthless. It is known
(see T. Jennings Wilson's *Love, Life and Hanky-panky at the Court of
Louis XIV*) that when the Sieur de Bienville presented himself at court
prior to sailing for the New World to take possession of his land grant
and knelt before His Majesty, the King said to him, "A word to the
wise, Jean-Phillipe, baby: don't come back; otherwise, you'll be the
Headless Horseman of the Bois de Boulogne."

Department of Alcoholic Beverage Taxation, and they were forced to retreat under a hail of small arms fire.

Through the good offices of the Archbishop of New Orleans, however, a meeting was finally set up (on neutral territory in Mississippi, Horsey having no faith in the solemn word of any elected or appointive official of the state of Louisiana) and negotiations were undertaken.

Horsey did not want a six-lane super highway running through his property at all, and it took considerable cajolery on the part of everyone else concerned to move him from this position.

It was finally agreed that he would be awarded sixty thousand dollars (this figure was described by the New Orleans *Picaroon-Statesman,* in a flaming editorial, as "an unconscionable rape of the state treasury") in exchange for a one-hundred-yard-wide right-of-way through his land, and his solemn promise not to shoot at the construction crews or otherwise interfere in any manner with the march of progress.

Although this was not known to anyone but the principals, Horsey turned over to Father Jacques de-Presseps, the Bayou Perdu parish priest,* substantially all of the highway department check, reserving for himself only enough money for a few essentials. He treated himself to a half-gallon bottle of Old White Stagg Blended Kentucky Bourbon, a delicacy he had remembered with yearning from the patients' club at the 4077th MASH; he gave his wife enough money to buy a new bonnet and a new dress; and he sent orders

---

* Father dePresseps, a French national, had been sent to Bayou Perdu from his native Normandy as a result of negotiations at the highest levels of the Church. His predecessor, an American priest of Irish extraction, had been found floating down the Mississippi River in a pirogue, babbling mindlessly about "crazy Cajuns and crosses to bear."

to Sears, Roebuck and Co. to ship him a new outboard motor for his pirogue and to come and drill him a new water well.

Normally, of course, the sudden influx of approximately fifty-nine thousand dollars to the parish treasury would not have gone unnoticed, and it would not have gone unnoticed here had not the Sears, Roebuck water-well drilling crew failed miserably in the accomplishment of their assigned duties.

They found not a drop of water. What they found, in the words of the *American Oil & Gas Journal,* was "the largest pool of natural gas ever discovered anywhere."

The first partial payment on the first royalty check came to slightly over $1.4 million. The next day, the Chancellor of the Archdiocese of New Orleans, Monsignor John Joseph Clancy, opened a letter bearing the return address of Saint Mary's Church, Bayou Perdu. A check for $140,000 fluttered out, the first in a long series of checks representing ten percent of the gross proceeds.*

While they were delighted with Horsey's (and their own) good fortune, both Monsignor Clancy and the archbishop privately feared that the sudden wealth would not be a good thing for the simple inhabitants of Bayou Perdu.

"However," the chancellor said to the archbishop, "it may not be a problem for long."

"What do you mean by that, Jack?" His Eminence inquired.

---

* Despite what some disgruntled Knights of Columbus of different councils have said, Horsey's tithing gifts to the archdiocese are not the reason the Bayou Perdu Council, K. of C., seems to enjoy both special privilege and the archbishop's favor. On the other hand, of course, it hasn't hurt their relationship, either.

"A Cajun and his money are soon parted," the monsignor said.

"I'm afraid you may be right, Jack," the archbishop agreed with reluctance.

He was wrong. His Eminence had either underestimated or misunderstood the character of both Cajuns and Normans. (He was, of course, an Irishman.) The greatest con men in the world tried, and failed, to part Horsey from his money. The combination of a Louisiana Cajun making business decisions with the advice of a Norman peasant priest was too much for them.

The archbishop's fears of conspicuous consumption on the part of Horsey and the Bayou Perdu Council, K. of C., were unfortunately and soon realized. The pilings were barely sunk for a new Saint Mary's Church (a somewhat enlarged and improved version of Saint Peter's in Venice) when construction of the new social hall for the Bayou Perdu Council, K. of C., began. No expense was spared. The New Social Hall, as it came to be called, had six bowling alleys, a swimming pool, an auditorium and the largest solid mahogany bar in the world.

The uniforms with which, B. H. G., the Bayou Perdu Council, K. of C., had been equipped had first seen the light of day in the 1939-40 New York World's Fair, where they had adorned the ushers. After the visit of a gentleman from Brooks Brothers Theatrical Costumes, Inc., the Knights were uniformed so splendiferously that they had to be seen to be believed, and even when seen they were rather unbelievable.

The Bayou Perdu Council, K. of C., Marching Band (originally three tubas, two bass drums, six Jew's harps and a glockenspiel), which had, frankly, been rather outshined by other K. of C. bands within the New Orleans consistory, was, after augmentation by a number of professional musicians,* without question the leader of the pack.

After a series of unfortunate highway mishaps when the fleet of new Lincolns and Cadillacs with which the Knights had replaced the two Model A's, one 1939 Buick, and two ex-school buses of the Bayou Perdu community proved too much (especially on the way home) for the Knights, Horsey got in touch with the people who make the Greyhound buses and ordered four of these vehicles, specially equipped.

The buses were equipped with seats identical to those furnished for first-class passengers on intercontinental jet aircraft. There were on-board bar and rest room facilities. The buses were painted bright yellow and had mounted on their roofs a cluster of silver-plated air horns, which, when the horn button was pressed, played "Onward, Christian Soldiers."

The initial delight experienced by upper-level management when the first ten rows of the fifty-yard section of seats were sold "in perpetuity" to a religiously based social organization without a quibble about the price was soon replaced with something less than the first blush of enthusiasm.

Not only did the other paying customers begin to register complaints that while they, as loyal New Orleanians, liked "When the Saints Go Marching In" as well as the next fellow, it did begin to grate on the nerves a little toward the end of the game, after it was played, in its entirety, by a one-hundred-six-piece band, heavy on the brass, not only every time the

* Horsey de la Chevaux had visited the governor, checkbook in hand, in the mistaken belief that the University of Louisiana Million-Dollar Marching Band was up for sale. The governor explained with such tact and grace that it wasn't for sale that Horsey wrote him a little check for his expenses in the next campaign. Shortly aferward, recognizing in former Sergeant de la Chevaux characteristics of military leadership and all-around tactical genius that the state should not have to do without, the governor appointed Horsey as Colonel of Infantry on his staff.

Saints scored a touchdown, but whenever the Saints tackled a member of the opposing team.

Moreover, it quickly became apparent that the reason the Knights were so anxious to be on the fifty-yard line, at ground level, was that from that location it was very convenient for them to race out onto the field and demonstrate with officials who had, in their opinion, come to the erroneous conclusion that a member of the Saints had somehow violated the rules.

After it was put to Horsey that an impasse existed (after visiting the hospital room of an official who had both of his shoulders dislocated by one of the Knights after he had made an unpopular call, the umpires' association had gone on strike with the announcement that they would not return to their duties until the Knights were somehow placed under control), the ground-level seats on the fifty-yard line were exchanged for enclosed, air-conditioned boxes high above the field. So that the fans would not be deprived of the musical offerings of the Bayou Perdu Council, K. of C., Marching Band, it was agreed that they would perform at half-time. It was also agreed, tacitly, that any official found on the field while the marching band was performing was fair game.

But it was the post-game social festivities that caused the most trouble. Chevaux Petroleum Corporation, International, in the interests of maintaining high employee efficiency through high employee morale, customarily arranged for what was described as an "employee banquet, dance and social."

Employees and their families were housed on a floor or two of the nearest suitable hotel; the hotel's Grand Ballroom was engaged for the banquet and dance, and lesser facilities were set aside and designated as the Ladies' Lounge, the Men's Bar and the Kiddies' Karrousel. Since it was not fair to expect a performance

by the Bayou Perdu Council, K. of C., Marching Band
(they were, of course, exhausted after playing at the
game), Papa Louis' Old-Tyme New Orleans Dixie-
land Jazz Band was customarily flown in from New
Orleans to provide a musical background.

A standing invitation to the Saints team and their
families to join in either the victory festivities or the
wake generally saw about half the team and their families in attendance, despite objections of the Saints'
management.

Much effort was expended by all concerned parties
to keep events, scheduled and unscheduled, under control. Normally, all this effort met with only limited
success. If it were possible, in other words, for something to go wrong, it usually did.

On one memorable occasion, in the Dallas Hilton,
for example, it did not come to the attention of responsible officials that the Texas Women's Christian
Temperance Union was holding its annual convention
in Ballroom A of the hotel until a delegation of
Knights, each clutching a half-gallon bottle of Old
White Stagg Blended Kentucky Bourbon, marched
into the meeting to the strains of Papa Louis' band
playing "Cigarettes, Whiskey and Wild, Wild Women"
in the belief that they were entering Ballroom B,
where a Miss Bonnie Bazooms was scheduled to offer
a display of her terpsichorean art.*

The point has been made. It would not be really
necessary to dwell at such length upon the subject were
it not for the fact that Mrs. Mary Pierce, wife to the
aforementioned Dr. Hawkeye Pierce, was (a) fully
aware of the legends surrounding the Bayou Perdu

* Miss Bonnie Bazooms' "Dance of the Pigeons," during which
specially trained pigeons cleverly removed one piece of her attitre at a
time, had, over the years, become almost as much a sacred tradition of
a post-game party as the reenactment of the Saints' successful touchdown
attempts in the lobbies of the various hotels.

Council post-game socials and (b) happened to learn that Esther Flanagan was going to the game.

Esther Flanagan, R.N., was a foot taller, thirty pounds heavier and twenty years older than Mary Pierce. Esther Flanagan, as has been previously reported, was also a retired naval officer who had spent twenty-odd years of her life following the flag to various exotic corners of the world. Despite this background, Mary Pierce, whose highest military rank had been neighbor chairgirl for the 1949 cookie sale of the Girl Scouts of America, and who had never traveled farther than fifty miles from her home unless accompanied by father, brother or husband, had come to the conclusion that Esther Flanagan was nothing but an innocent girl about to find herself in a situation fraught with unspeakable (at least in mixed company) danger.

Esther Flanagan, R.N., liked Mary Pierce. She liked her so much, in fact, that she did not laugh in her face when Mary came to her and suggested, ever so tactfully, that it might not be a very good idea for Nurse Flanagan to go so far from home alone to be among people who were not, as Mary phrased it, "really very nice," and whose "standards of behavior," as she put it, were "a little odd."

"It's all right, Mary," Esther Flanagan said. "I'll be safe with Hot Lips."

"It's not that I don't *like* the Reverend Mother Emeritus," Mary said. "But, frankly, I can't help but wonder sometimes what someone called 'Hot Lips' did before, so to speak, she got the call."

"I'm going to the game, Mary," Esther Flanagan said gently but firmly. "All work and no play, to coin a phrase, makes Esther Flanagan hard to live with."

"I hope you didn't think, Esther," Mary Pierce said quickly, "that I thought you, of all people, would do something wrong."

"Not at all," Esther said.

Fifteen minutes later Mary Pierce broached the subject to her husband.

"If you think I'm going to let you let Esther Flanagan go to New Orleans and Texas alone, Hawkeye, you've got another think coming!"

"You're going with her? Great idea!"

"Bite your tongue! I'm the mother of your children! How could you even suggest such a thing?"

"A passing moment of madness," Hawkeye said. "Well, then, what?"

"Well, then, what, what?"

"If you're not going to go with her, who is?"

"You are," she said firmly.

"I am not. I'm the father of your children! How could you even suggest such a thing?"

"You and Trapper John are both going," Mary announced with finality. "Lucinda* and I have talked it over."

"What's sauce for the gander should be sauce for the goose," Hawkeye said. "What you're proposing, Mary, is sexual discrimination, pure and simple! The next thing you'll be doing is expecting me to open doors for you, hold out your chair and such other disgustingly discriminating acts! Possibly even tip my hat!"

"Shut up, Hawkeye," Mary said.

"I can't go to Texas, Mary, as much as I would like to," Hawkeye said piously. "I have things to do around here—doctor things. I have, you know, sworn solemnly to serve my fellowmen in their hours of medical difficulty."

"I thought of that," she said. "And I know how

---

* Dr. John Francis Xavier McIntyre has been for some years united in the blessed bounds of matrimony with a lady named Lucinda. Lucinda and Mary Pierce are what is known in feminine circles as "best friends."

much you were looking forward to your turn on the D.D.D.* schedule."

"Perhaps, after all," Hawkeye said, "I can tear myself away for a couple of days."

"I thought you'd come around," Mary said.

"But aren't you and Lucinda worried," he asked, curiosity having overcome his common sense, "about Trapper John and me getting in trouble with the Knights?"

"Esther will be there," Mary said quickly. "She'll keep an eye on you."

"Of course," Hawkeye replied. Long years of marriage had taught him that one does not try to deal reasonably with one's wife or even attempt to understand her thought processes. One simply chooses the path of least resistance. This is known as husbandly wisdom.

---

* In a noble attempt to drive the last vestiges of sexism from the classroom, the Spruce Harbor Elementary School Parent-Teacher Association had come up with a plan whereby, on a rotation basis, each male parent (or "Daddy") would serve as a (female) teacher's helper for one school day. The designation cleverly selected to describe this operation was D.D.D., for Daddy's Day of Duty.

Chapter Five

As this conversation was taking place in Spruce Harbor, another member of what sometimes is referred to as the gentle sex examined a 22-by-28-inch photograph through large, canary-yellow-framed pink tinted glasses and made an announcement.

"They're darling!" she said. "Just darling! Both of them! Lance, you're fantastic!"

"I thought you'd be pleased," Lance said. Lance Fairbanks had taken the photograph of which the lady approved. He smiled, and after running his index finger over his right eyebrow, he put his hand on his hip and called out, "Brucie, would you bring in the others now, please?"

While Lance Fairbanks' voice was not at all unpleasant (it had a certain lilt to it), it could not accurately be described as heavily laden with what our Latin-American friends refer to as "machismo."

Compared to him, as a matter of fact, when the lady

with the purple hair and the canary-yellow-framed pink tinted glasses asked, "Oh, you have more? Wonderful!" she sounded like Telly Savalas.

"I have oodles and oodles," Lance Fairbanks replied. "Brucie and I were up all night slaving and slaving in the darkroom!"

Brucie came (perhaps "floated" would be a more accurate description of the way he moved) into the room, a small and precise little man attired in crushed velvet blue jeans, sandals and a horizontally striped T-shirt that was patterned after those worn in the French Navy. The chartreuse silk ascot around his neck matched the chartreuse silk scarf he wore in lieu of a belt to hold up the crushed velvet blue jeans.

He carried in his outstretched arms a stack of at least twenty-five photographs, each as large, about two feet square, as the first one the lady had seen, and of which she had so gushingly approved.

He laid them on a fire-engine-red table with all the élan of a liveried lackey setting, for example, a roast suckling pig before Catherine the Great of Russia. The simile is not farfetched. The lady with the purple hair was Sydney Prescott, founder, president and absolute mistress of Sydney Prescott & Associates, Advertising. She was known as the "Queen Bee of New York Advertising," an appellation making reference both to her gender and her sting.

Lance and Brucie stood back as Ms. Prescott went through the photographs. She went through them carefully, holding each one up in both hands for a moment, then laying them in three stacks.

When she had finished, she turned to face Lance and Brucie, her back to the plate-glass wall, which offered a view of New York City, generally, and Park Avenue and the Pam Am Building, specifically, behind her.

She extended one long and rather bony finger to-

ward one of the stacks of photographs. The finger carried a twelve-carat square-cut diamond that had once
adorned the finger of the czarina of all the Russias.

"These are good," she said. She moved her finger,
the nail of which was adorned with metal-flaked purple nail polish, to the second stack. "These are better."
Lance and Brucie sort of swayed in ecstasy at her approval. "And these, darlings," she said, smiling
broadly and pointing to the third, largest and last
stack, "are simply awful!"

The smiles Lance and Brucie had been wearing
vanished and they advanced somewhat timidly to look
down at those that she disapproved of.

"I see what you mean," Lance Fairbanks said.

"You're right, of course," Brucie chimed in.

"I'm always right," Sydney Prescott said. "Now, tell
me where you shot these."

"In the wilds of Texas," Lance said.

"You're kidding!"

"Would I kid you, Sydney?" Lance inquired.

"Not unless you suddenly lost your senses," Sydney
Prescott replied.

"Far from the frontiers of civilization," Brucie
chimed in again.

Sydney Prescott went to the second stack, the photographs she had said were "better," and she went
through the half a dozen photographs it contained. She
finally selected one of these, walked to an azure-blue
corkboard mounted on her wall and stuck one of the
photographs on it with glass-tipped thumbtacks.

The object of her approbation showed two male
human beings. They were squatting on the heels on
their battered cowboy boots beside a campfire. Two
pie-bald ponies, their reins hanging loosely to the
ground, stood behind them. One of the men had his
leathery face decorated with a somewhat shaggy mus-

tache, matching the shaggy gray hair that stuck out from beneath a somewhat soiled ten-gallon hat. He was attired in a tight-fitting shirt, from the breast pocket of which hung the string of a package of roll-your-own cigarette tobacco, and well-worn jeans.

The other man, of a somewhat darker hue, was similarly attired, down to the package of tobacco in his pocket (in his case, chewing tobacco), except that he had no mustache, and in lieu of a ten-gallon hat he had a feather sticking out of his hair, held in place by a band of leather tied across his forehead. He had a large knife jammed into his belt. The one with the mustache had a large Colt-.45 single-action revolver stuck in his belt.

They were both in the act of eating from tin plates. Beside them on the ground were two cans of a product called Wild West Beanos.

"And you actually got them to eat the Wild West Beanos!" Sydney Prescott said excitedly. "Lance, you really are fantastic!"

"It was nothing, really," Lance Fairbanks said modestly.

"Tell mother all," Ms. Prescott said, "from the very beginning!"

"Well, there we were," Lance began, "miles and miles from nowhere, so to speak, riding through the desert in our little Winnebago, and then Brucie spotted them."

"Brucie spotted them?" Sydney Prescott inquired.

"Brucie said, 'Lance, will you look at that?' And I looked where he pointed, and there they were."

"Where were they?"

"Riding through the desert," Lance went on, "leading a buffalo on a rope."

"A buffalo on a rope? But I don't see any buffalo in the pictures."

"I gave it some thought," Lance said, "a great deal of thought. And I thought that there was such a thing as being *too* authentic. I mean, are a cowboy and an Indian *and* a buffalo credible?"

"I see your point," Ms. Prescott said.

"So we drove over and tried to strike up a conversation," Lance said.

"Lance," Brucie amplified, obviously very impressed with his friend's behavior, "just jumped out of the Winnebago and said, 'Hi, there, I'm Lance Fairbanks.' "

"And what did they say?"

"It didn't go too well at first, to tell you the truth," Lance said.

"What do you mean?"

"Well, Sitting Buffalo—that's the Indian, his name is Sitting Buffalo—said, 'Screw you, White Man,' and he spit tobacco juice over the Winnebago's windshield. It must have been a good ten feet, too."

"And then the cowboy took out his gun," Brucie said, visibly excited at the memory, "and cocked it, and pointed it right at Lance and said, 'We shoot trespassers in these parts, fella.' "

"My God!" Ms. Prescott said.

"But Lance rose to the occasion," Brucie said, pride in every syllable.

"What did he do?"

"He made believe he fainted," Brucie said. "The minute the cowboy pointed the gun at him, he went down like an express elevator."

"Good thinking, Lance," Ms. Prescott said. "Then what?"

"The next thing I remember," Lance said, "I mean, when I pretended to be waking up from pretending to have fainted, Sitting Buffalo was pouring water on my face."

"I see."

"So then I told them that we weren't really trespassing, but that we were lost," Lance went on. "And he said that was a shame, because if we were lost then he couldn't shoot us."

"But how did you get them to eat the Wild West Beanos?" Ms. Prescott asked. "*That's* the important thing."

(It is necessary at this point, to maintain the continuity of this narrative, to parenthetically explain not only what Lance and Brucie were doing running around west Texas in their Winnebago and to tell something of the history of Wild West Beanos, but also to explain the interrelationship of Lance and Brucie, Wild West Beanos and Sydney Prescott & Associates, Advertising. The explanation follows:

(Long before Sydney Prescott left J. Walter Batten-Barton, Advertising, Inc., to form Sydney Prescott & Associates, Advertising—in fact, long before Sydney Prescott had changed her name from Sadie Prausnitz —she had had her dream. Unlike others of her gender, however, however, her dream had nothing to do with cohabiting in a vine-covered cottage by the side of the road with a handsome knight in shining armor mounted on a white horse.

(Sadie's dream, even then, was to have for her very own the advertising business of Babcock Burton & Company. Babcock Burton & Company were in the tobacco game. They manufactured seven brands of cigarettes, fourteen brands of cigars, five brands of chewing tobacco and, for those who frowned on burning and chewing the filthy weed, four brands of snuff.*

---

* For the uninitiated, there are two kinds of snuff. One kind is removed from the can, believe it or not, by a pinch of the fingers and is then placed in a soggy ball in the mouth, between the teeth and the lip. The other kind is placed on the back on the hand and sucked into the nostrils with a healthy inhale. The snuff industry is not at all amused by the phrase "up your nose with a rubber hose."

(Babcock Burton & Company were firm believers in advertising. Stripped of taxes, it cost Babcock Burton & Company just under fifteen cents to deliver a package of cigarettes to the "final vendor." Of that fifteen cents, just under ten cents was spent buying tobacco (or growing it themselves on their vast farms), drying it, roasting it, chopping it up into little pieces, making cigarettes out of it, wrapping the cigarettes and trucking them across the country. The balance of their cost, a little over a nickel a pack, was spent on advertising.

(There was a similar cost breakdown for other products. Four cents of the pre-tax eighteen cents that an Old Dutchman Corona cigar cost was set aside for advertising, and every time a snuff-dipper laid out his fifty-nine cents for a tin of Old Mountain Lion, Babcock Burton & Company plowed 8.9 cents right back into advertising.

(The advertising game works on a percentage of the money spent on advertising, and Sadie Prausnitz was still learning the ropes in the mailroom of J. Walter Batten-Barton, Advertising, Inc., when she computed that 8.9 cents times four million tins of Old Mountain Lion (not to mention the cigars, cigarettes and chewing tobacco) was a hell of a lot of money.

(One could not, of course, simply walk into the North Carolina corporate headquarters of Babcock Burton & Company, ask to speak to Mrs. Babcock Burton III, Presidentress and Chairperson of the Board, then announce that you wanted to handle their (more accurately, *her*) advertising. With such a pot of gold at the bottom of the Babcock Burton & Company rainbow, there was a lot of competition.

(It took years for Sadie Prausnitz, by then Sydney Prescott, to get inside the Babcock Burton & Company corporate headquarters with an advertising proposal that even slightly interested the most junior assistant manager of relatively unimportant product advertising.

(But, finally, to quote from *Advertising and Little Me*, Sydney Prescott's autobiography, she was "given the chance," and a contract was let for Sydney Prescott & Associates, Advertising, to assume advertising responsibility for one of the lesser Babcock Burton products, Old Billy Goat Snuff. Recognizing that opportunity had knocked at her door, and that it was unlikely to knock again, Ms. Prescott decided to devote the full efforts of Sydney Prescott & Associates, Advertising, to Old Billy Goat Snuff, to the exclusion of all other activity. Her cousin Maxwell was called down from his "ivory tower"* to lend his efforts to the project, which could make or break her newborn and heavily mortgaged agency.

(Sydney Prescott had noticed, with professional interest, an advertising campaign, mounted with some success by a competitor, which informed potential female cigarette customers that they had come, in Sydney's quaint little paraphrase, "a long distance, Süssl."

(She had already learned, at J. Walter Batten-Barton, Advertising, Inc., the two sacred principles of advertising, to wit: "Nothing Succeeds Like Success" and "Imitation Is Cheaper Than Imagination." Thus, she was able to mount her first campaign with relative ease.

---

* At the time, Max Prausnitz, Sadie's paternal cousin, was drawing the public's attention to the fine products offered by Smiling Sam Shapiro's Pre-Owned Motor Salon. When called to the Old Billy Goat Snuff project, he had been atop Mr. Shapiro's flagpole, the highest in the Bronx, for thirty-six days, and the full-length dress and blonde Marilyn-Monroe wig in which he was attired were, frankly, getting a little ratty. But, although Mr. Prausnitz modestly declines to talk about it, he does hold the Bronx flagpole-sitting record for female impersonators atop flagpoles over thirty-five feet.

(Lance Fairbanks, a brilliant photographer whom Maxwell Prausnitz had met on the sand dunes of Fire Island, whence he had gone to commune with nature, and who was fortunately at liberty at the time, was thus able to go to work not only immediately, but on what Ms. Prescott described in her book as "a delayed compensation basis."*

(Among Elroy Finley/Lance Fairbanks' social acquaintances was a rather tall young lady whose biological response to the male gender was every bit as wild and uncontrollable as Elroy/Lance's biological response to the female gender.

(One afternoon, when they were sitting around the lady's apartment killing time by doing each other's hair, inspiration struck. Without even waiting for the Clairol Ash-Blonde to complete its work, Lance jumped up from his chair and posed the lady, whose name was Fern, but who preferred to be called "Fred," against a poster for the Folies-Bergère, which Fred had hung there to conceal a hole in the plaster.

(In that now famous shot, Fred, attired in a denim shirt open to the belly button and a pair of cut-offs, held a can of Old Billy Goat Snuff so that the label could be clearly seen in her left hand, and she held her right hand, palm down, under her nose, in the manner of snuff sniffers.

(Lance immediately developed the film and printed

---

* As Ms. Prescott put it to him at the time, "Elroy, you get yours when and if." What she meant by this was that Mr. Fairbanks (still using, at that time, the name he was born with, Elroy Finley) would be compensated for his photographic endeavors when Sydney Prescott & Associates was paid by Babcock Burton & Company. The "if" was included in her statement because the cold truth was that she had not actually received a *contract* from Babcock Burton & Company to handle Old Billy Goat Snuff. What she actually had w⸺ ⸺promise from the junior assistant manager of relatively unimportant ⸺ ⸺ advertising, whom she had trapped in an elevator, "to look at whatever she came up with." But, as Ms. Prescott always says at the slightest provocation, "If you can't trust Babcock Burton, whom can you trust?"

it in 11-by-14-inch format. The prints were dried with
Fred's hair drier, and Lance rushed out of the apartment to have the copy lettered onto the film.*

(The photograph of Fred, in her cut-offs and denim
shirt, sniffing snuff while looking directly at the camera
lens, and over the one, short, brilliant line of copy, "Up
Yours, Honey!' " won the Kevin Farrell Award for
Advertising Genius—"The Kevvie"—at the annual
advertising profession banquet.

(While the approbation of one's professional peers
was, of course, stimulating, more important was the
check from Babcock Burton & Company, which ac-
companied the contract that gave them actual responsibility for the entire advertising campaign for Old
Billy Goat Snuff. The check was for forty-five hundred
dollars, representing six percent of the previous year's
gross sales, seventy-five thousand dollars, of Old Billy
Goat Snuff.

(In what was described as a stroke of genius, Ms.
Sydney Prescott spent the entire budget to have Lance
Fairbanks' photo of Fred sniffing snuff reproduced on
oversized bumper stickers. She and Fred then spent
long hours affixing them to mirrors in ladies' rest
rooms in Y.W.C.A.'s, Y.W.H.A.'s, singles bars and in
certain Greenwich Village saloons recommended by
Fred. Giving credit where credit is due, it was Fred
who conceived the notion of offering the "Up Yours,
Honey!" sticker/posters for sale in various "in,"
avante-garde and women's lib publications.

(The rest, of course, is advertising history. Sales of
Old Billy Goat Snuff skyrocketed overnight. Within
months Olde Billie Goat** was selling as much in thirty

---

* As Lance reported later, he knew that the gods were smiling on his
idea when a handsome chap answered his knock at the door of his shop,
Greenwich Village Calligraphy Salon and Signs Painted. The handsome
chap, of course, was Brucie.

** The change in name and spelling was Fred's idea.

days as it had sold in twelve months, and when the campaign went national, sales exceeded even Ms. Sydney Prescott's wildest expectations.

(The result was a major shake-up of the advertising policies of the Relatively Unimportant Products Division of Babcock Burton & Company. Longtime advertising agencies were given an unceremonial heave-ho, and the work was reassigned to Sydney Prescott & Associates.*

(But Ms. Prescott was still no closer to getting her hands on the really lucrative cigar and cigarette accounts than she ever had been, and there seemed to be absolutely nothing she could do about it.

(And then there intervened what Sydney Prescott thought of as "fate" and what Mrs. Babcock Burton III thought of as "[expletive deleted] governmental interference with the free enterprise system."

(Cigar lovers, incurable readers of fine print and the insatiably curious, but few others, are sometimes aware of an announcement placed in the smallest available print in the most obscure position on many cigar boxes. This announcement reads: "These Cigars Are Predominantly Natural Tobacco with Non-Tobacco Ingredients Added." This somewhat horrifying announcement is printed on the boxes at governmental decree, following what the government considered to be a far too liberal interpretation on the part of cigar manufacturers of what actually constituted tobacco.

(There is more to a tobacco plant than leaves, just as there is more to a corn plant than succulent yellow kernels. In the not unreasonable belief that, since the ultimate consumer was going to burn the product rather than eat it, he (or she) would be unlikely to

---

* The Associates now included, of course, Lance and Brucié and Fred, who was given the title of Executive Creative Consultant, although she continued to be the model for the Olde Billie Goat account.

notice the difference, cigar manufacturers began to include in their product first the tough vein that runs down the center of the leaf; then the stem that affixes the leaf to the stalk; then the stalk itself. When the cigar manufacturers were discovered by an official variously described as "a miserable government snooper" and "a dedicated public servant" to be washing off the roots, then chopping them up for inclusion in the final product, the cry of "Enough is enough!" was heard, and the little line about non-tobacco products became required on cigar products.

(Babcock Burton & Company, which was recognized as a leader of the industry, had gone even further in interpreting the word "tobacco." They came to the conclusion that anything green that grew in a tobacco field was, *per se* and *de facto*, tobacco.

(Among the things that grow in tobacco fields are weeds and various other plants, including a variant of *Soja hispida. Soja hispida* is, of course, the common soybean, described by some as one of God's better beans. The variation of *Soja hispida* (*Soja hispida Burtonosis*, to be specific) growing in Babcock Burton's North Carolina fields, however, was not your ordinary run-of-the-mill soybean. For one thing, it produced, compared to the other, standard, soybean, very little oil. For another, the only vegetable killer that worked on it was even more effective on tobacco plants.

(This posed no real problem for long years. *Soja hispida Burtonosis* was simply roasted, toasted, ground up and included in Babcock Burton's cigars. And then the dedicated public servants/miserable bureaucrats spoke again. "Henceforth and forever more," they said (or words to this effect), "no more *Soja hispida Burtonosis* in cigars, even with a disclaimer."

(What the government had learned, after extensive

tests, at God only knows what cost to the taxpayer, was that while there wasn't very much oil in the bean of *Soja hispida Burtonosis*, what there was, when burned, like when ground up in a cigar, was nearly identical, chemically speaking, to JP-4 fuel. JP-4, for the uninitiated, is sort of a low-grade kerosene used to run jet engines.

(In the belief that the cigar smoker should not be inhaling the smoke from not-entirely consumed JP-4 fuel, the prohibition was issued, and no amount of money, no matter how liberally dispensed in the halls of Congress, saw the prohibition lifted.

(The result was that enormous piles of *Soja hispida Burtonosis* began to grow around Babcock Burton & Company's tobacco warehouses. For some time, the North Carolina skies were dark with black clouds of smoke rising from enormous (haystack size) piles of burning *Soja hispida Burtonosis*. Then the Environmental Protection Agency jumped into the act, saying that the smoke was not only interfering with the ozone layer in the stratosphere, but making people throw up as far away as Winston-Salem, and that it had forced the 82nd Airborne Division to give up practice parachute-jumping at Fort Bragg. The burning was ordered stopped.

(It was at this point that Mrs. Babcock Burton III, after due deliberation, with her senior staff of executives gathered nervously before her satin wood desk in her oak-paneled office, took desperate action.

("Send for that nutty advertising broad from New York," she said.

("Right, B.B.," one of her executives said. "Immediately!"

("Which nutty advertising broad was that, B.B.?" another executive asked.

("The one who looks like Bella Abzug and has all

the old maids sniffing snuff," Mrs. Babcock Burton III replied. "If she's crazy enough to come up with an idea like that, she's liable to have an idea about this [expletive deleted] *Soja hispida Burtonosis*.")

Chapter Six

(In the belief that news of failure serves to do nothing but feed discouragement, Mrs. Babcock Burton III had not told her senior executive staff that she had just had news of failure. Her son, Babcock Burton IV, had telephoned only an hour before the emergency meeting to report that none of the pigs on the Babcock Burton Experimental Farm would eat *Soja hispida Burtonosis*, no matter what he did to it, and so far he had tried grinding, cracking, boiling, steaming, mashing and, just for the hell of it, mixing it with pig feed.

("No use, Mother," Babcock said. "They won't touch it."

("Never say die, dear," Mrs. Burton replied, then hung up.

(*Soja hispida Burtonosis* aside, Babcock IV, known to his friends as "Bubba," was Mrs. Burton's greatest problem. A mommy of the old school, she believed

71

it was high time that her first and only born should
find the right girl and settle down in the home of his
choice, either the villa in Santa Monica, the apartment
in New York, the ski lodge in Vail, the *pied-à-terre*
in London or, for that matter, right there in the cottage
in Burton, North Carolina. While Mrs. Burton was
aware that two families should not share one roof,
she wasn't entirely sure the rule applied to the cottage, whose roof covered one hundred twenty-eight
rooms on three floors.

(He was, after all, old enough. He was twenty-
two. She herself had married his father, then nine-
teen, when she was sixteen, and the memory of the
four years of their marriage, before Babcock Burton
III had, in his cups, fallen off the yacht, was her most
precious possession.

(Bubba, in some ways, was just like his father.
He was tall and blond and handsome, with a sturdy
body and firm white teeth. And, like his father, he was
just a shade wild. Like Daddy, he had quit college and
run away from home. But Daddy had run away to get
married, and Bubba had run away to join the army.
He had spent three years as a sergeant in the Green
Berets and then had come home with the announcement that, now that he had seen the world, all he
wanted to do henceforth was run the farm.

(But, unlike Daddy, Bubba didn't spend all of his
time chasing girls. Quite the reverse. He spent most
of his time avoiding them.

("Mother," he had told her when she brought the
subject up as tactfully as she knew how, "things have
changed since your era of long ago. It is now the
girls who chase the boys, and while I find the attention paid me flattering, I want to be something more
to the girl I ultimately marry than a sex object. Besides, I'm still young. Let me enjoy my innocent

youth sky-diving with my pals over at Fort Bragg; let
me spend as much time as possible with my pigs,
while there is still time. Before you know it, the cutest
piglet is an eight-hundred-pound boar. And, really, I
am much too young to pledge my heart to any one
girl."

(Although it was costing Babcock Burton & Company more money than Mrs. Babcock Burton III,
whose first name was Josephine, liked to think about,
she was in a way pleased that the problem vis-à-vis
Soja hispida Burtonosis had come up. It was the first
corporate problem in which Buba Burton had shown
the slightest interest. She was as sorry that feeding the
pigs with what she thought of as "that goddamned
bean" had proved a failure for Bubba in his first
attempt to solve a corporate problem as she was that
it hadn't done a thing about the mountains of beans
that grew by the day.

(And so Josephine Burton was willing to listen to
any suggestion, however wild, from whomsoever,
however weird, had one.

(She was not prepared for the idea, however, that
sprang from the purple-lipsticked lips of Ms. Sydney
Prescott as soon as the problem had been put to her.

("Why don't you commission Sydney Prescott &
Associates," Ms. Prescott had replied without a moment's hesitation, "to come up with a nice little
package, and a campaign for the package, of course,
and sell this stuff for people to eat?"

(Bubba, like his father, always liked a good laugh,
and so Josephine Burton had, right then, put in a call
to him at the farm. He was finally located on a
tractor, and the conversation was carried on through
the modern miracle known as C.B.:

("Pigman, this is Little Momma. Got your ears
on? Come back."

("Ten-four, Little Momma," Bubba replied. "What's your Ten-twenty? Come back."

("Little Momma's at work, Pigman, with Weird Yankee Beaver. Come back."

("Little Momma, Pigman's told you to stop finding beavers for me."

("This isn't that kind of a beaver, Pigman. This is a funny beaver."

("What kind of a funny beaver? Come back."

("This one wants us to sell *Soja hispida Burtonosis* as food for humans."

("What's so funny about that, Little Momma?"

("Pigman, you told Little Momma yourself that the pigs won't eat it," Josephine Burton said. "Come back."

("Little Momma, Pigman has told you and told you that pigs are smarter than people. Your funny beaver may have something. Come back."

("You really think so, Pigman?"

("Ten-four, Little Momma. Give her a shot at it. Seventy-threes to you and the funny beaver. Pigman going Ten-ten and standing by. King-king-queen, Seven-zero-one-zero, Mobile Unit Four, out."

(Ms. Sydney Prescott was given a carte blanche contract that very afternoon to develop a campaign to get rid of the goddamned bean by selling it as food for human consumption, together with an understanding that if she were successful, Babcock Burton & Company would look upon her company with "special favor" when it came time to award advertising contracts for Babcock Burton & Company cigars and cigarettes.

(Ms. Prescott and her associates discarded the first notion that came to them, that of selling *Soja hispida Burtonosis* as a snob food under some terribly chic trade name. Even after Lance came up with some ter-

ribly chick photographs of Fred, roller-skating topless
through United Nations Plaza and waving *Soja hispida
Burtonosis* vines joyfully above her head, which simply
deserved to be on the cover of *Cosmopolitan,* they
realized they couldn't go through with it.

(Foisting off what even Ms. Sydney Prescott had
come to think of (privately, of course) as "that goddamned bean" on unsuspecting New York sophisticates
and intellectuals would really be a loathsome thing to
do.

("Very infra dig," as Lance, who was into things
British, said. "Letting the side down, don't you know?"

(It was then, perhaps inevitably, that the idea came
to feed *Soja hispida Burtonosis* to those who were
not New York sophisticates and/or intellectuals.
The idea, on its very face, had merit. For one thing,
there were far more of these people than there were
New Yorkers, and there were a hell of a lot of beans
to get rid of. For another, as every New Yorker knows,
anyone who chooses to reside south of Brooklyn,
north of the Bronx or (especially) west of the Hudson
River is not very bright and would more than likely
slurp up with delight anything put on his or her plate,
just so long as it didn't smell too bad and came with
a catchy name.

(For reasons that absolutely baffled Ms. Sydney
Prescott, most people outside New York, as well, truth
to tell as many bona fide Manhattanites, were absolutely fascinated with things of the Old West. Ms.
Prescott thought of this as the "John Wayne syn-
drome," and she was aware that a competitive cigarette
manufacturer had done very well pushing his product
by associating it in the consumer's mind with Longhorn
cattle and leathery-faced cowboys.

("Lance," she ordered, "go West! And don't come

back until you've got the cowboy's cowboy. I want him to simply *reek* of the West."

("What's that got to do with anything?" Lance replied. "Or *Soja hispida Burtonosis?*"

("Never say that name again," Ms. Sydney Prescott said. "That goddamned bean is dead! Wild West Beanos is born!"

(Here ends the parenthetical explanation of what Lance and Brucie were doing running around west Texas in their Winnebago, and why.)*

"But how did you get them to eat the Wild West Beanos?" Ms. Prescott asked. *"That's* the important thing."

"When I have to be, Sydney," Lance said, "I can be very persuasive!"

Ms. Prescott was examining the photographs again.

"I see what you mean," she said. "It isn't very believable."

"What isn't very believable?" Lance sort of snapped.

"The buffalo," she said. "You got him, or it, in one of these pictures."

"I just wanted you to see for yourself, Sydney," Lance said. "The cowboy and the Indian alone sort of strain one's credibility. When you add the buffalo, it's just too, too much."

"Well, Lance," Sydney Prescott said, "you and Brucie get right back out there just as soon as you can and sign these two ugly, if native American, peasants to a contract. I'm going to make them famous!"

"I'm not going anywhere," Lance said, "until Fred has a chance to do my face and hair!"

"We all must be prepared to make little sacrifices,

---

* The astute reader may have noticed that the parenthetical explanation took in a number of pages and parts of two chapters. This was not entirely by accident, the authors having no better way of getting themselves listed in the *Guinness Book of World Records* than by composing the world's longest parenthetical explanation.

Lance," Sydney said. "Take Fred with you if you want, but get your little ass back to the Wild West!"

"I will not!" Lance said, stamping his Gucci loafer firmly on the thick black-and-orange carpet.

"Lance, you could take some wonderful pictures of Fred out there," Brucie said. "I can see her now, on the desert at sunset, sitting sidesaddle on that buffalo, with the Indian holding its rope."

"Perhaps you have something," Lance said after a moment.

"And in the meantime I'll send these pictures down to Mrs. Babcock Burton III," Ms. Prescott said. "They'll prove to her that Sydney Prescott & Associates are well on the way to solving the bean problem."

The response from Mrs. Babcock Burton III to the photographs was not what Ms. Sydney Prescott had expected. There was a telephone call from a Southern gentleman of great charm and tact. It came over Sydney Prescott's Number Three unlisted number, so she knew it was someone important.*

"Hello!" she snapped.

"Good afternoon, ma'am," the cultured, deep Southern male voice said.

"What number are you calling?" Ms. Prescott snapped, not recognizing the voice and naturally coming to the conclusion, as a New Yorker, that the caller was either seeking a charitable donation or offering, for example, a course in ceramic ashtray-making at The New School.

---

* Unlisted numbers are as essential to New York advertising biggies as, say, pencils and paper clips. Ms. Prescott had three unlisted numbers. Number one, which was connected to the switchboard, was given to unimportant people. Number two, which was answered by her secretary, was given to middle-level biggies. Number three, which she actually answered herself, was given out only to upper-level biggies, including her cousin Maxwell and Lance Fairbanks, but not to people like Brucie and Fred.

Her caller gave the correct number.

"Do I know you? Who are you?" Ms. Prescott demanded.

"My name is J. Darrell Kenyon, ma'am," he said.

"Never heard of you," she said. "Get to the point, Mac. I'm a busy lady."

"I am calling at the request of Mrs. Babcock Burton III, ma'am."

"Mr. Kenyon," Ms. Prescott said, "how *good* of you to tear yourself away from your busy, and I *know* how *important,* schedule to call little old me. How may I be of some small assistance to you?"

"I just this moment heard from Mrs. Babcock, ma'am," Mr. Kenyon said. "She communicated with me from the Babcock Burton Experimental Farm via what I believe is known as Citizen's Band, or C.B. radio. Are you familiar with this mode of communication, ma'am?"

"A little," Ms. Prescott replied. This was untrue, but she was not the sort of person who readily admitted ignorance of any subject.

"Splendid!" he said. "I confess that it sometimes is a bit much for me. I therefore habitually take the precaution of tape-recording all messages. Perhaps if I played it back for you, you might be able to make something out of it."

"Well, we'll give it the old school try, Mr. Kenyon."

"What old school is that, ma'am?"

"Brooklyn Polytechnic," Ms. Prescott replied.

"I didn't think you sounded as if you'd gone to Duke," he said. "Please stand by."

There was a faint hissing noise, then:

"Little Momma, King-king-queen, Seven-zero-one-zero, Mobile Unit Four to Base. You got your ears on?"

"Come back, Little Momma," a female voice replied. "You got the Typewriter Kid."

"Typewriter Kid, this is Little Momma speaking. I'm out here on the tractor with Pigman. I just showed him the pictures that Weird Yankee Beaver sent down from Dirt City. You copy?"

"Ten-four, Little Momma," the female voice replied.

"Pigman lays a big Ten-four on the pictures," Little Momma continued, "a great big Ten-four. So I want you to get Kenyon and tell him to get on a land line to Weird Yankee Beaver, and tell Weird Yankee Beaver to get right back to me with the Ten-twenty of the photographer so that Pigman can meet them. You copy? Come back."

"I think so, Little Momma," Typewriter Kid replied. "Pigman wants the Ten-twenty of the photographer so he can join up with them. Ten-four? Come back."

"That's a big Ten-four, Typewriter Kid," Little Momma replied. "And while he's doing that, you get on a land line to the airfield and have them warm up a plane. One of the little jets would do nicely. Pigman'll be alone. You copy?"

"That's a big Ten-four, Little Momma."

"Get right on it, Typewriter Kid. King-king-queen, Seven-zero-one-zero, Mobile Unit Four, Little Momma, going Ten-ten."

The hissing stopped.

"As well as I am able to judge, ma'am," Mr. J. Darrell Kenyon said, "Mr. Babcock Burton IV, after having examined some photographs, has not only made his approval known, but wishes to join the photographer, presumably to supervise additional photography. Would that seem a reasonably rough translation to you, ma'am?"

"I would think so," Ms. Prescott replied.

"Then the only problem I have, ma'am, is contacting Weird Yankee Beaver. I have only this number, and Typewriter Kid's . . . I mean, Miss Howell's . . . description of her."

"What was that?"

"A good-looking Bella Abzug," Mr. Kenyon replied. "Could you help me, ma'am?"

"I'll get right back to you, Mr. Kenyon," Ms. Prescott said. "Sydney Prescott & Associates, as one more service to its valued clients, always knows precisely where its staff may be located at any given time. Just as soon as I locate Weird Yankee Beaver, I'll telephone you and let you know where the photographers are."

"I'll be waiting for your call," Mr. Kenyon replied. "Thank you so much."

Ms. Prescott picked up another of the telephones on her desk even before she got the one she already had in her hand back in its cradle.

"Find out what they call the states between here and Texas," she ordered. "And get me, one at a time, the chief of the state police in each of them."

"Is something the matter, Ms. Prescott?" her secretary asked.

"You bet there is," Ms. Prescott replied. "Lance Fairbanks' wife and their triplets have just been in a terrible automobile accident, and we have to get word to him."

"Lance Fairbanks' *wife?*" the secretary replied, somewhat incredulously. "And their *triplets?*"

"You'd better change that," Ms. Prescott said on second thought. "Say Lance Fairbanks accidentally forgot to take his heart pills with him, and unless we get the pills to him, he's liable to die—unless, of course, the state police can find that Winnebago. It shouldn't be hard to find. There aren't many lavender Winnebagos out there with 'Gay Power' bumper stickers."

Forty-five minutes later Ms. Prescott got back to Mr. Kenyon with the information that Mr. Fairbanks was at that very minute awaiting further orders at the Marysville, Arkansas, municipal airport.

And an hour after that a small jet aircraft appeared in the azure-blue sky over Marysville.

"That must be him," Lance Fairbanks said to Brucie and Fred. "You notice how the jet engine contrail spells out 'Smoke Babcocks'?"

"I am very much afraid that he will turn out to be one of those crude types of men who likes women," Fred said, "one of your typical male chauvinist sexist pigs."

"Sydney said we were to expect that," Lance said, "and that we were to remember that as backward and as unenlightened as he might be, his Little Momma is paying the bills, and it's hands-off time."

"If that pilot expects to land that *gorgeous* little jet on this dinky little airfield, he'd better start slowing down," Brucie observed professionally. (Before he had gone into the sign-painting game, he had been an airline steward.)

The pilot of the little jet did not slow down. He made a pass over the field at six hundred miles per hour at two hundred feet, then pulled up sharply to about five thousand feet, slowing down as he did so.

"What was all that about?" Fred asked. Then she quickly said, "Look, it broke. A piece just fell off."

The piece fell toward the earth as the plane, gathering speed and altitude, sped off toward the horizon. And then a white canopy suddenly appeared in the sky.

"Oh, my!" Brucie said.

And then the strains of "The Tennessee Waltz,"* sung in a jubilant basso profundo, were heard floating down from beneath the parachute. Moments later it appeared that the parachutist was going to land right on top of them. Lance and Brucie, holding tightly onto one another, dropped to their knees. Fred was too startled to do anything.

The parachutist landed lightly on his feet, then gathered the chute in his arms.

"Hello," he said, "I'm Bubba Burton."

"Do you always get off airplanes that way?" Fred asked.

"Whenever possible, ma'am," Bubba Burton replied. He looked at Lance and Brucie, who were in the process of getting to their feet.

"You must be Mr. Lance Fairbanks," he said.

"Oh, yes!" Lance replied in one enormous sigh.

"Oh, my!" Brucie said.

"I was afraid Mother would be right about you," Bubba said. "But I don't see where it's going to be a problem."

"You don't?"

"I met your kind in the army," Bubba said, "mostly in the Quartermaster Corps. But once they understood the rule, we never had any trouble with them."

"What rule was that?"

"If they came closer than six feet, we broke their legs," Bubba said.

"You'll have no trouble with me, Bubba," Lance said quickly. "Six feet it is."

"It might be worth it," Brucie mused, then quickly added, "but duty before pleasure, as I always say."

"Well, let's get this show on the road," Bubba Burton

---

* The parachutist was actually singing the version sung by the 8th Special Forces group, stationed in Germany: "I was waltzing with my *Schatz*, East of Eschwege," *etc*. But Lance, Brucie and Fred were in no condition to notice the difference.

said. "People sometimes get upset when they hear my name, so the way we'll play it is that I'm the driver of that Winnebago and my name is Bubba Jones. Understood?"

"Perfectly," Lance and Brucie said almost in unison.

"My name is Fern," Fred said. "And I'll bet you're just a *great* driver."

"You mean 'Fred,' darling," Lance Fairbanks corrected her. "Tell Bubba your name is 'Fred.'"

"Mind your own business, you lousy pansy," Fern said, taking Bubba's arm and allowing him to help her enter the Winnebago.

Chapter Seven

Three airplanes were parked outside the International Arrivals and Departures Building* of Abzug International Airport. One of them was a droop-nosed, supersonic, French-built Le Discorde. It had just arrived on the morning run from Paris, bearing the day's freshly baked French bread, and it was about to depart. It was experiencing minor mechanical difficulties. The batteries were low, and the pilot was reluctant to shut down the engines. Since the rate of fuel consumption, at idle, was only five percent lower than the fueling rate of the fuel truck, refueling the sleek silver bird had turned out to be a lengthy process.

The second airplane was an American-built ship, a Douglas DC-9 bearing both the insignia of Air Hussid

---

* The International Arrivals and Departures Building at Abzug International Airport was the only building at the airfield, for the very good reason that Abzug had only one airfield, and aircraft (save those flying in circles, of course) arriving or departing were, *ipso facto*, on international runs.

and the personal colors of His Royal Highness Prince
Hassan and Kayam, heir apparent to the Hussidic
throne, and Ambassador Extraordinary and Pleni-
potentiary to the French Republic, the Court of Saint
James and the United States of America. It, too, when
fueled, was Paris-bound, carrying His Royal Highness and Boris Alexandrovich Korsky-Rimsakov,
the world's greatest opera singer.

The third aircraft was a Boeing 747 jumbo jet,
bearing the legend CHEVAUX PETROLEUM CORPORA-
TION, INTERNATIONAL on its fuselage and two flags on
its enormous vertical stabilizer. One flag bore the Stars
and Stripes, and it was crossed with the official flag
of the Bayou Perdu Council, Knights of Columbus.

The fuel tanks of the 747 were more or less full,
with more than enough fuel to carry the ship to its
destination, Spruce Harbor International Airport,
Maine. It seemed, however, simple courtesy to Col.
Jean-Pierre de la Chevaux that he delay his departure
until the departure of His Royal Highness and Mr.
Korsky-Rimsakov, especially since the cards were running his way.

The peculiarly American game of chance, known to
the cognoscenti as seven-card stud, was being played
in the forward cabin of the 747. Participants were:
Colonel de la Chevaux; His Royal Highness Prince
Hassan ad Kayam; Mr. Korsky-Rimsakov; a long and
lithe young lady, Esmerelda Hoffenburg, prima bal-
lerina of the Corps de Ballet of the French National
Opera in Paris; and His Royal Highness Sheikh Abdullah ben Abzug, Sheikh of Sheikhs, Protector of the
True Faith, the Lion of Abzug and Honorary Knight
Commander of the Wheel of Chance, Bayou Perdu
Council, K. of C., whose insignia he wore proudly
(together with the one-hundred-two-carat Star of Ab-

zug diamond) to affix the golden ropes of royalty that held his burnous to his head.*

"Read 'em and weep," the Sheikh of Sheikhs, Protector of the True Faith, *etc., etc.,* said, laying down a spade flush, queen high.

"Jesus H. Christ!" Mr. Korsky-Rimsakov said, a hint of annoyance in his booming voice. "I knew I was making a mistake when I taught you how to play this game!"

"Up yours!" the Sheikh of Sheikhs, *etc., etc.,* said with a broad smile, sweeping in the pile of money. He smiled at each of his fellow players in turn and

---

* Those interested in grand opera, as well as those interested in the international oil business, will doubtless be curious as to how come the world's greatest opera singer and the president of the board of the Chevaux Petroleum Corporation, International, not only happened to be playing seven-card stud with His Most Islamic Majesty, Shiekh Abdullah ben Abzug, but, whom, exactly, His Most Islamic Majesty happens to be.

Scholars are directed to *M*A*S*H Goes to Morocco* (Pocket Books), in which all the somewhat sordid details have been recorded in what has been described as "a very unusual style, indeed."

For the purposes of understanding this narrative, however, it is probably sufficient for the reader to know that His Most Islamic Majesty is absolute ruler of the kingdom of Abzug, which is located "somewhere south of Morocco" (the boundaries have never been agreed upon) and which contains, in addition to 2,300,000 loyal subjects of His Most Islamic Majesty, 1,500,000 goats, 200,000 camels, a couple of dozen lions, tigers and other exotic fauna, plus oil and natural gas reserves second only to those of Saudi Arabia.

His Most Islamic Majesty and Mr. Korsky-Rimsakov became friends in Paris, France, where Mr. Korsky-Rimsakov taught His Majesty his first words of English at a four-day *fête d'été* (or summer festival) of the Parisian Business Girls' Marching & Chowder Society held at the apartment occupied by certain members of the U.S. Marine Guard of the Paris Embassy. As a token of his admiration for both his singing ability and his performance with the membership of the Parisian Business Girls' Marching & Chowder Society, it pleased His Most Islamic Majesty not only to grant Abzugian citizenry to Mr. Korsky-Rimsakov, but to raise him to the Abzugian nobility as El Noil Snoil the Magnificent, Privy Councillor to the Throne. In his role as Privy Councillor, Mr. Korsky-Rimsakov recommended to His Most Islamic Majesty that the Chevaux Petroleum Corporation be granted the Royal Seal as oil and gas producers to H.R.H. Sheikh Abdullah. His Majesty accepted the recommendation, and he and Colonel de la Chevaux became close personal friends.

repeated the phrase "Up yours!" with each gracious nodding smile of the royal head. The others were not annoyed. They were aware that His Royal Highness spoke little English and that he had learned what little he knew from Mr. Korsky-Rimsakov.

The door to the cabin opened, and a tall, distinguished-looking Arabian gentleman entered, dressed in flowing robes of the finest silk. He dropped to all fours and then approached the Sheikh of Sheikhs on his knees. He made a gesture of subservience. The Sheikh of Sheikhs made an impatient gesture, and the distinguished Arabian gentleman rose high enough on his knees to whisper in the Sheikh of Sheikhs' ear.

A look of sad inevitability crossed the face of the Lion of Abzug. He dismissed the messenger with a regal wave of his hand, and the messenger backed out of the royal presence on all fours.

"The bread plane has been fueled," the Sheikh of Sheikhs announced.

"Just in time," Mr. Korsky-Rimsakov said. "If this game had gone on any longer, I would have had to sing twice this month, and I don't like to wear myself out."

Mr. Korsky-Rimsakov rose, took Miss Hoffenburg's arm and spoke his farewells. "Thanks for nothing, Abdullah," he said to His Royal Highness, Sheikh of Sheikhs, *etc., etc.* "Take care, Horsey. Give my love to Hot Lips," he said to Colonel de la Chevaux.

"Isn't there time for one more little hand?" Sheikh Abdullah asked rather plaintively.

"Sorry," Boris said, "I'm singing tomorrow, and I need my exercise. You know that. Come on, Hassan, let's go!"

There was a bone-chilling roar as Le Discorde raced down the runway and soared aloft, looking, as Mr.

Korsky-Rimsakov* often said, like a "goosed vulture."

The door of the aircraft opened. Mr. Korsky-Rimsakov stepped out on the platform atop the stairs. The Band of the 2nd Squadron, Royal Abzugian Cavalry Corps, struck up "The Star Spangled Banner," paying "honors" to Mr. Korsky-Rimsakov, and Mr. Korsky-Rimsakov** stood there solemnly at attention, with his hand over his heart, until the music was finished.

His Royal Highness Prince Hassan ad Kayam next stepped onto the platform at the top of the stairs. The band struck up the Hussidic national anthem. They had played but six bars when Mr. Korsky-Rimsakov suddenly made a cutting motion with his fingers against his throat.

"Knock it off!" he shouted. The band died, as they say, not with a bang, but a whimper. "That's the trouble with you, Hassan. You really go for stuff like that. A little modesty is what you need. Pattern yourself after me."

He started down the stairs, Prince Hassan, and then Miss Hoffenburg followed him, and they were then transported by Jeep to the DC-9. Horsey de la Chevaux and Sheikh Abdullah ben Abzug, *etc., etc.,* stood at the top of the stairs and waited until the Air Hussid aircraft had taken off.

Then Horsey turned to Abdullah and put out his hand.

---

* Mr. Korsky-Rimsakov, who stood six-feet-six in his bare feet, did not like to fly on Le Discorde aircraft, whose cabins were six-feet four-inches high. On several sad occasions, he had forgotten himself and stood erect for one reason or another.

** The honors rendered to Mr. Korsky-Rimsakov were for his *alter ego* function as El Noil Snoil the Magnificent, Privy Councillor to the Throne. "The Star Spangled Banner" was played because the Abzugian national anthem hurt Mr. Korsky-Rimsakov's ears.

"Take care of yourself, ol' buddy," he said. "I gotta get going, too."

"I have a little farewell present for you, my beloved and highly respected friend," the Sheikh said.

"I don't want a present!" Horsey said quickly and in alarm. But it was too late. Sheikh Abdullah had already snapped his fingers. The present was ushered, with much girlish giggling, from where it had been waiting in the shade under the wing.

"A baker's dozen," His Royal Highness said with a grand gesture, using another of his few English phrases. "Hot to trot!"

Colonel de la Chevaux responded in Abzugian, one of the rarer tongues, consisting essentially of grunts and wheezes, with a belch-like sound for emphasis.

"I've told you and told you, my wife won't let me keep virgins," he said. "Our house isn't big enough."

The Sheikh looked crestfallen. "How about just one?" he asked. "I had these sent all the way from Algeria."

"Not even one," Horsey said. "I've told you that before. It is a taboo in our country. When we have virgins, we try to marry them off—when they're still in that condition. We don't pass them out like chocolate candy to our friends."

His Royal Highness just looked at Horsey. Tears welled up in his eyes. One ran down his suntanned cheek to lose itself in his thick, pure white beard.

"Stop that, Abdullah," Horsey said. "Tears will get you nowhere."

"I was only trying in some small way to show you the depth of my respect, admiration and affection," His Royal Highness said. Tears now ran down both cheeks.

"What do you really want?" Horsey said, suddenly understanding the whole thing.

"In return, you mean? Why, nothing at all, absolutely nothing at all," His Royal Highness said. "I understand completely your total ignorance of good manners, your cold and callous infidel heart, and that you find absolutely nothing at all wrong with leaving someone who loves you like a brother alone here, with all of his friends flying away to the far corners of the world."

"In other words, you're trying to sucker me into taking you along to the Saints-Cowboys game, is that it?"

"I accept," His Royal Highness said, suddenly grabbing Horsey de la Chevaux by both arms picking him twelve inches off the floor and kissing him wetly on both cheeks. He turned to the keeper of the royal virgins, speaking in the excitement of the moment in English. "Ditch the broads!" he ordered. He set Horsey back down, marched into the 747, and spoke again, again in English: "Hubba-hubba, let's get this show in the road!"

Horsey shrugged in the Gallic manner, and he followed His Royal Highness inside the airplane. As the door closed, the outside port engine came to life.

Before the 747 could taxi to the end of the runway, a message flashed out from the Royal Abzugian Telephone & Telegraph radio-telephone facility atop Mount Abzug:

FROM ROYAL ABZUGIAN FOREIGN MINISTRY
TO ROYAL ABZUGIAN EMBASSY
WASHINGTON, D.C.

FOLLOWING TO BE DELIVERED IMMEDIATELY BY AMBASSADOR TO U.S. SECRETARY OF STATE:

BE ADVISED THAT HIS MOST ISLAMIC MAJESTY, SHEIKH ABDULLAH BEN ABZUG, SHEIKH OF SHEIKHS,

PROTECTOR OF THE TRUE FAITH, THE LION OF ABZUG, MAY HIS TRIBE INCREASE, MAY HIS ENEMIES DEVELOP BOILS ON THEIR REPRODUCTIVE ORGANS, HAS MOST GRACIOUSLY, AS A TOKEN OF THE ESTEEM IN WHICH HE HOLDS YOURSELF, THE PRESIDENT OF THE UNITED STATES, AND YOUR LOYAL SUBJECTS, CONDESCENDED TO AFFORD THE UNITED STATES THE FAVOR OF HIS PRESENCE. HE HAS THIS DATE DEPARTED FOR THE UNITED STATES, WHERE IT IS HIS MOST ISLAMIC MAJESTY'S GRACIOUS INTENTION TO FAVOR THE NEW ORLEANS SAINTS-DALLAS COWBOYS FOOTBALL GAME WITH HIS AUGUST PRESENCE.

THE CIRCUMSTANCES OF HIS MOST ISLAMIC MAJ-ESTY'S DEPARTURE WERE SUCH THAT HE IS NOT AC-COMPANIED BY EITHER HIS HAREM OR HIS PERSONAL BODYGUARD. THE BODYGUARD WILL DEPART FOR THE UNITED STATES JUST AS SOON AS THE AFTERNOON SNAIL-AND-PRESSED-DUCK FLIGHT FROM PARIS ARRIVES AND IS UNLOADED. THE HAREM'S TRAVEL PLANS HAVE NOT BEEN FINALIZED AT THIS TIME.

IN THE INTERIM, IT IS PRESUMED THAT YOUR GOVERN-MENT WILL TAKE ADEQUATE SECURITY MEASURES TO PROTECT HIS MOST ISLAMIC MAJESTY FROM HARM. THE AIRCRAFT THAT HIS MOST ISLAMIC MAJESTY HAS FAVORED WITH HIS PERSON WILL STOP AT SPRUCE HARBOR, MAINE, AND NEW ORLEANS, LOUISIANA, BE-FORE PROCEEDING TO DALLAS.

IN THE NAME OF SHEIKH ABDULLAH BEN ABZUG, SHEIKH OF SHEIKHS, ETC., ETC. END MESSAGE. ADVISE DELIVERY.

MOULAY BEN HASSAN
FOREIGN MINISTER

Just as soon as the 747 reached an altitude that permitted Colonel de la Chevaux to use the single-side-band radio-telephone transceiver to call the United States, he placed a call. The miracle of radio-telephone communication connected him to the Spruce Harbor Medical Center, where he spoke with Dr. Benjamin Franklin Pierce, the chief of surgery.

"Hi-ya, Hawkeye," he said.

"What's on your mind, Horsey?" Hawkeye replied.

"Just called to tell you we'll be there about midnight."

"What do you mean, 'we,' you crazy Cajun?"

"I got Abdullah with me," Horsey replied.

"In words of short syllables, Horsey, go away!"

"Hawkeye, I didn't have the heart to tell him no," Horsey said. "He was standing there with tears running down his cheeks into his beard."

"Look, I'm in enough trouble around you without that crazy Arab . . . and his harem . . . and his bodyguard . . ."

"No bodyguard, Hawkeye. No harem."

"How'd you work that?" Hawkeye asked suspiciously.

"Believe me, Hawkeye, there's nobody on the plane but Abdullah and me."

"I got it," Hawkeye said after a moment's thought. "Boris and Hassan and the harem and the bodyguard are on another plane, right?"

"Boris and Hassan are in Paris," Horsey said. "They're not even going to the game. And the harem and the bodyguard are in Abzug. Honest."

"Cross your heart and hope to die? K. of C. word of honor?"

"Absolutely," Horsey replied.

"In that case, okay," Hawkeye said. "We'll meet you at the airport at midnight."

"See you then," Horsey said and hung up.

He looked around the forward cabin. Abdullah was

nowhere in sight. But Horsey knew immediately where to find him. He went into the main cabin, and there he was, a broad smile on his face, his hands folded on his back, his robes and burnous flapping in the breeze he stirred up as he roller-skated around the main cargo cabin, empty save for a couple of Caterpillar D-8 tractors, to the strains of "The Emperor's Waltz" on the public address system.*

"Horsey, put on some skates," His Royal Highness said. "We can play a little two-man hockey."

"Not right now, Abdullah," Horsey said. "Roll over here. I've got a great idea for you."

Abdullah did as he was told, skating over with rather graceful movements and sliding to a halt.

"You ever wonder what it would be like to be an American?" Horsey asked.

"My compassion for the poor and downtrodden is bottomless, Horsey," His Royal Highness said. "Of course I have."

"How would you like to be an American for a couple of days?"

"No way," His Royal Highness said. "I said I was compassionate, not masochistic."

"You said you wanted to give me a present," Horsey said.

"Name it," His Royal Highness said. "It's yours!"

"I want you to get rid of the bathrobe and that towel on your head for a couple of days, Abdullah," Horsey said, "and wear regular clothes. Forget that you're a sheikh."

"Why?" His Royal Highness asked rather pointedly. "What kind of a present is that?"

---

* The aircraft, after having delivered oil-well equipment and technicians to the Chevaux operation in Nigeria had been en route home, virtually empty, when diverted to Abzug to pick up Colonel de la Chevaux, who had gone to Abzug from Paris with Prince Hassan ad Kayam and Mr. Korsky-Rimsakov.

"Let's say I owe a favor to a friend," Horsey said. "And I can pay it back that way."

"What friend?"

"Dr. Hawkeye Pierce," Horsey said.

"The one *Cher* Boris calls the Sainted Chancre Mechanic?"

"That's the one."

"I like him," His Royal Highness said. "I will do it. Or I will try to do it. But it will be of no use whatever for me to disguise myself as an infidel. We Sheikhs of Sheikhs, you know, are not like ordinary people."

"By the time I get through with you, Abdullah, even your wives won't recognize you," Horsey said. He picked up the telephone connecting to the cockpit.

"Hey, Jack," he said to the pilot, "get on the horn and find the nearest place we can rendezvous with a smaller plane—one of the Sabreliners, for example. And then ask Ernie to come down here a minute. I need a favor."

It took Ernie, who was the flight engineer, several minutes to climb all the way down from the cockpit to the main cargo compartment and then walk all the way back to the locker room and showers. But it was immediately apparent why Horsey had sent for him. Ernie was nearly as large as His Royal Highness.

"Ernie, I need to borrow some clothes for my friend," Horsey said, "and you're the only guy anywhere near his size."

"Gee, Horsey," Ernie said, "I'd like to help you out, but I was on vacation doing some surfing when they picked me up in Hawaii. I don't have much with me."

"Whatever it is, it'll be better than Abdullah's bathrobe and towel," Horsey replied. "Go get it."

Chapter Eight

Meanwhile, back at the ranch:

Ida-Sue Jones could see through the Plexiglass window as her helicopter approached Uncle Hiram's ranch that at least one thing was going well. She saw the long black limousine in which she had dispatched Eagle Eye MacNamara to the university to get Scarlett. It was now, at her orders, meeting her at the ranch.

And when, apparently when they heard the fluckata-fluckata-fluckata sound of the helicopter rotors, MacNamara came outside the log cabin, followed by two other men, she deduced, correctly as it turned out, that her other orders had been complied with. MacNamara had brought with him an attorney at law and a duly licensed medical doctor specializing in the practice of psychiatry.

Eagle Eye MacNamara rushed to the helicopter as soon as it touched down, ducking his head to avoid having it sliced off by the still-turning blades.

"Well, you finally did something right, I see, Eagle Eye," Ida-Sue greeted him.

"I think it would be a good idea if I had a few words with you, Mrs. Jones," Eagle Eye said.

"Are those two clowns the shrink and the shyster, or not?" she snapped.

"They are," Eagle Eye said. "But there's something . . ."

"Shut up, Eagle Eye," Ida-Sue said. "Time's a wasting." Revealing what seemed, even in these times, to be an extraordinary amount of black-lace-trimmed thigh, Ida-Sue climbed down from the helicopter and advanced on the medical and legal gentlemen Eagle Eye had brought with him. (The amount of thigh and unmentionables she had placed on display was intentional. If she had learned nothing else while serving as a University of Texas Marching Band Pom-Pom Girl, it was that nothing will catch and hold a man's attention more effectively than a woman's legs and underpants.)

The two gentlemen were wide-eyed.

"Mornin', ma'am," they said, raising their Stetsons and speaking almost in unison.

"Hello, gentlemen," Ida-Sue said, flashing each of them in turn a dazzling smile, and allowing each to touch, very briefly, her hand before she snapped it back. "Aren't you *nice,*" she went on, "to come *way* out here heah on the prairie to see little me!"

"My pleasure, ma'am," the taller, fatter, and more red-faced of the two replied, bowing with great grace, considering his waistline. "Andrew Jackson Stewing, M.D., F.A.S.P.P., at your service, ma'am."

"FA.S.P.P.?" Ida-Sue asked, curiosity having gotten the better of her.

"Fellow," Dr. Stewing said with quiet pride, "American Society of Practicing Psychiatrists, ma'am."

"How darlin'!" Ida-Sue said. "A pleasure and an honor, Doctor."

"My friends, little lady, call me 'Fat Jack,'" the psychiatrist confided.

"I'll bet they do!" Ida-Sue replied, then turned to the other gentleman, who was considerably thinner, but of about the same height.

"And you, sir," Ida Sue declared, "must be Mr. Croshett."

"Begging your pardon, ma'am," he said. "We pronounce that in the French manner, 'Cro*shay*.' And if you don't mind, ma'am, it's *Dr*. Richard Crochet, L.L.D., Attorney and Counselor at Law, at your service, ma'am."

"How interesting!" Ida-Sue said. "As I heard my husband, the Congressman, say just the other day, 'If it weren't for lawyers and psychiatrists, where would we all be?'"

"He certainly has a point, ma'am," Dr. Stewing replied. "Now, how may we be of service?"

"Well, I suppose you have met Uncle Hiram," Ida-Sue said as she took a hanky from her purse and dabbed at her eyes. "Poor, poor Uncle Hiram."

"No, ma'am," Attorney Crochet said. "We have not had that privilege."

"We've just been standing around here with Mr. MacNamara and admiring your uncle's shaggy cows," Dr. Stewing said. "I don't believe I've ever seen this breed before."

"They're not *exactly* cows, Doctor," Ida-Sue said. "They're buffaloes, actually."

"I knew that all the time," Attorney Crochet said.

"*Buffaloes?*" Dr. Stewing asked incredulously. "Buffaloes? Like they used to have on the nickel?"

"Isn't that crazy?" Ida-Sue replied with a little laugh. "I mean, isn't that *insane?*"

"I would say it's carrying nostalgia a bit far," Dr. Stewing said. "Probably the owner had too strict toilet training as a child."

"I'm sure he did," Ida-Sue said. "I'm sure you could tell that just by looking at him, being an F.A.S.P.P., I mean." She turned to Eagle Eye MacNamara. "Where is poor, poor Uncle Hiram, Eagle Eye?"

"I'm afraid he's not here, Mrs. Jones," Eagle Eye MacNamara replied. "That's what I was trying to tell you before."

"What do you mean, he's not here?" she snapped. "Uncle Hiram never leaves the ranch. He sits here in this lousy log cabin, sitting on top of the largest proven oil reserves in west Texas, and he does nothing but drink rot-gut whiskey with his Indian pal and raise buffaloes."

"Did I understand you to say, ma'am," Attorney Crochet said, "that there is oil under this prairie?"

"Yes, there is," Ida-Sue said. "And I live in fear that unscrupulous persons may cheat Uncle Hiram out of it, him being a little crazy and all, you understand."

"Pardon me, ma'am," Fat Jack Stewing said, "but we psychiatrists frown upon simple lay persons such as yourself, ma'am, making judgments about other people being crazy. That's our business."

"What I was hoping," Ida-Sue said, "when I asked you gentlemen to meet me here to discuss this problem was that you might be able to help poor, crazy Uncle Hiram."

"What exactly did you have in mind, ma'am?" Attorney Crochet said.

"Well, since money is no object, Uncle Hiram having six million dollars that I know about in a bank, not even to think what all the oil under here is worth, I was hoping that you might be able to recommend to me some dedicated practitioner of the law who would, say for ten percent off the top, manage Uncle Hiram's affairs for him—with my advice, of course—while he is off getting the best psychiatric care money can buy, even if his case is hopeless and he has to spend the rest of his days in some comfortable institution."

"There's only one problem, ma'am," Fat Jack Stewing, M.D., F.A.S.P.P., said.

"And what is that, Doctor?"

"In order to get your lunatic uncle locked up in my private psychiatric hospital, we have to find him."

"Which brings us back to you, Eagle Eye," Ida-Sue said. "Where is he?"

"I don't know," Eagle Eye confessed. "I stopped for gas and to ask directions, and the guy at the gas station told me there was no point in coming out to the Old Bar X, because Hiram wasn't here."

"Did he say where he was?"

"He said he saw him driving down the highway in his pickup, with Teddy Roosevelt in the back and some sexy blonde up in front with him and Sitting Buffalo."

"*Who* was in the back?" Ida-Sue asked.

"I'm just telling you what the guy said, Ida-Sue, and what he said was 'Teddy Roosevelt was in the back,' and Sitting Buffalo and some sexy blonde was up front with Uncle Hiram. As a matter of fact, now that I think about it, he said the sexy blonde was driving."

"My God!" Ida-Sue said, her face ashen, her voice shaking. "All I need now is for some peroxide-blonde hussy to snatch the old codger away, just when I finally figured out how to handle him."

"I wonder who she is," Eagle Eye MacNamara said. "Why would a sexy peroxide-blonde want to marry crazy Uncle Hiram?"

"Because under Texas law, you jackass," Ida-Sue said, "the wife gets control of the financial affairs of a crazy husband. In other words, the moment this gold digger marries Uncle Hiram, she gets not only fifty percent of all of this as community property, but also control of what he has left."

"I see what you mean," Eagle Eye said. "But what about Teddy Roosevelt? What's he got to do with all this? I thought he was dead."

"Under Texas law," Attorney Crochet said before Mrs. Ida-Sue Jones had the opportunity to reply to Mr. MacNamara, "marriages are invalid if either of the parties is *non compos mentis*."

"There you go again, using one of my profession's private little phrases," Fat Jack Stewing snapped. "Stay in your own backyard, Counselor. From what the little lady tells us, there's enough of Hiram's money to go around for everybody."

"What I was saying was that if either of the parties is either crazy or drunk," Attorney Crochet said, "the marriage is invalid."

Ida-Sue looked at him thoughtfully for a moment.

"That's a very interesting legal point, Counselor," she said. "But it won't hold water."

"What do you mean?"

"If the marriages of all the people I know who got married plastered were invalid, there would be more . . . I believe the Latin phrase is *illegitimit* . . . illegitimate children in Texas than anywhere else." The meaning of what she had just said sunk in. She quickly changed the subject.

"Did this gas station where you asked directions have a telephone, Eagle Eye?"

He nodded.

"Get in the car, everybody!" Ida-Sue ordered. She pushed the chauffeur out of the way and got behind the wheel herself. Bouncing wildly on the unpaved dirt road, the limousine headed back for the highway.

Thirty minutes later Teletypes in police stations all over Texas began to clatter:

FROM HEADQUARTERS, TEXAS RANGERS
TO ALL LAW ENFORCEMENT AUTHORITIES IN TEXAS

BE ON THE LOOKOUT FOR AND DETAIN THE FOLLOWING GROUP OF PERSONS:

(1) HIRAM DALRYMPLE, WHITE MALE, APPROXIMATELY SIXTY YEARS OF AGE, GRAY HAIR, GRAY BEARD, 180 POUNDS, LAST REPORTED WEARING STETSON HAT, DENIM SHIRT, DENIM TROUSERS AND BOOTS. IS PROBABLY ARMED WITH COLT-.45 SINGLE-ACTION REVOLVER.

(2) SITTING BUFFALO, INDIAN MALE, APPROXIMATELY SIXTY YEARS OF AGE, BLACK HAIR, RED COMPLEXION, LAST REPORTED WEARING FEATHER, DENIM SHIRT, DENIM TROUSERS AND BOOTS. IS ALSO PROBABLY ARMED, EITHER WITH WINCHESTER MODEL-1894-.30-.30 OR BOW AND ARROW, OR BOTH.

(3) TEDDY ROOSEVELT, DESCRIPTION UNCERTAIN, BUT PROBABLY EITHER WHITE OR INDIAN OR BLACK MALE OF SAME AGE, PROBABLY DRESSED IN APPROXIMATELY THE SAME WAY AND PROBABLY ARMED. SINCE HE WAS LAST REPORTED RIDING IN BACK OF TRUCK (DESCRIPTION FOLLOWS), HE IS PROBABLY EITHER INDIAN OR BLACK.

(4) WHITE FEMALE, NAME UNKNOWN, DESCRIBED AS THE SORT OF CHEAP PEROXIDE-BLONDE HUSSY WHO WOULD TRIFLE WITH A POOR OLD MAN'S AFFECTIONS. SUBJECT IS DESCRIBED AS YOUNG, WELL-TANNED, LONG-HAIRED, AMPLY BOSOMED AND DRESSED IN STETSON HAT, DENIM SHIRT, DENIM TROUSERS AND BOOTS.

THE PARTY WAS LAST SEEN TRAVELING IN THE GENERAL DIRECTION OF DALLAS IN A 1948 FORD PICKUP TRUCK, RUSTY IN COLOR AND MISSING FRONT

AND REAR FENDERS. SUBJECT DALRYMPLE IS UNDER THE PSYCHIATRIC CARE OF ANDREW JACKSON STEWING, M.D., F.A.S.P.P., BUT WILL PROBABLY DENY THIS. ON DETENTION, SUBJECT DALRYMPLE IS TO BE SEPARATED FROM OTHER MEMBERS OF THE PARTY UNTIL ARRANGEMENTS CAN BE MADE FOR HIS TRANSFER TO THE STEWING TRANQUIL GLADES REST HOME & DRYING-OUT SPA IN MIDLAND. OTHER SUBJECTS ARE TO BE RELEASED, PRESUMING NO WANTS OR WARRANTS ARE OUT FOR THEM, AFTER BEING WARNED THAT IT IS AGAINST THE LAWS OF THE GREAT STATE OF TEXAS TO AID, ABET OR HARBOR A LOONY.

THE HEAD TEXAS RANGER HIMSELF HAS TAKEN A PERSONAL INTEREST IN THIS CASE, AND ALL REPORTS ARE TO BE SENT TO HIM IN CARE OF THE TEXAS RANGER MOBILE DISASTER COMMAND POST, PARKING LOT B, TEXAS STADIUM, DALLAS, WHERE HE WILL BE UNTIL AFTER THE DALLAS COWBOYS-NEW ORLEANS SAINTS FOOTBALL GAME. FOR GENERAL INFORMATION, THE LOONY IS THE UNCLE OF MRS. IDA-SUE DALRYMPLE JONES, WIFE OF CONGRESSMAN ALAMO JONES, WHO HAS JUST ESTABLISHED THE WALLINGTON T. DOWD LAW ENFORCEMENT SCHOLARSHIP AT THE UNIVERSITY OF TEXAS IN HONOR OF THE FINEST TEXAS RANGER OF ALL TIME, OUR OWN BELOVED "WALLY" DOWD.

> BY ORDER OF WALLINGTON T. DOWD
> HEAD TEXAS RANGER

As the sleek, black (if somewhat dusty and with two hubcaps missing after the bumpy trip to the paved road) limousine carrying Mrs. Alamo Jones, Eagle Eye MacNamara, Andrew Jackson Stewing, M.D., and Richard Crochet, L.L.D., raced to the telephone at the Longhorn Café, Bar-B-Que & Texaco, it passed a Winnebago going in the other direction.

"Will you look at that!" Dr. Crochet said to Dr. Stewing.

"I'll be damned! Excuse me, ma'am," Fat Jack Stewing said.

"I never thought I'd see a house on wheels going that fast," Dr. Crochet said.

"*I* never thought *I'd* see a house on wheels painted lavender," Dr. Stewing said. "The owners obviously have problems."

"Probably a bunch of damned Yankees," Ida-Sue said, "down here causing trouble."

Not far from where it had encountered the Cadillac limousine, the Winnebago suddenly slowed down, leaving black streaks down the highway, and turned off at a sign reading OLD BAR X. NO TRESPASSING. SURVIVORS WILL BE HANGED.

"You're sure this is the place?" Bubba Burton Jones asked.

"I'm sure it is," Lance Fairbanks said. "I remember all those piles of buffalo do-do."

"They call them 'chips' out here, fella," Bubba said. "You can cook your supper on them. I mean, *I* could cook *my* supper on them. You probably would make a mess of it."

"Oh, Bubba," Fern said, "you know everything!"

"I'm going to throw up again," Brucie said.

"There it is," Lance said as the Winnebago skidded around the last turn and the log cabin came into sight. "It's so unspeakably quaint and picturesque."

"Pretty nice," Bubba said. "I could hardly have done it better myself." Then he reminded, "Don't forget the six feet, pal."

"Sorry!" Lance said quickly and retreated to the back of the Winnebago.

Bubba stopped the Winnebago in front of the log cabin and nimbly jumped out.

"Howdy!" he called out. There was no reply.

"Maybe there's nobody here," Fern said, joining him.

"I think I'll have a little look around," Bubba said. "You wait here."

In five minutes he was back. He climbed behind the wheel of the Winnebago, started it up and headed back in the direction they had come from.

"Where are we going, if I might be so bold as to inquire?" Lance called from the back of the Winnebago.

"To the Dallas Cowboys-New Orleans Saints football game," Bubba replied.

"But I thought you wanted to see those two wonderful, smelly old men," Lance replied.

"I do," Bubba answered. "That's why I'm going to the football game. That's where they are."

"How could you *possibly* know *that?*" Brucie asked.

"I'm a former Green Beret, you know,"* Bubba replied. "We have our little techniques."

"Oh, I'll bet you do!" Brucie said.

"A word to the wise, Brucie," Lance said. "I personally don't think he's fooling one little bit about what happens if you break the six-feet rule."

"Make that eight feet, you nauseating fruitcake, you!" Fern called back.

And as darkness fell slowly over the lavender Winnebago, making its way down a straight and narrow Texas highway toward Dallas, a sad little scene was taking place by the side of the road on the outskirts of Dallas.

---

* What had happened, actually, was that Bubba had come upon a discarded envelope, which Ida-Sue and the others had ignored, and upon which was written: "S., Here are the tickets you wanted to the Cowboys-Saints game. You and your uncle have a good time. B." As a faithful fan of the Saints, Bubba had, of course, the schedule committed to memory, and was thus able to cleverly hypothesize the probable whereabouts of this missing buffalo rancher.

"Him gone," Sitting Buffalo said. "The Great Spirit has left."

Tears ran down the cheeks of Hiram Dalrymple, and he swallowed hard.

"You take Princess Long Hair," Sitting Buffalo said. "I do it for you."

"No," said Hiram Dalrymple, his voice now firm. "I'll do it. I'd rather have it that way."

He pulled the well-oiled Colt-.45 single-action revolver from his belt, thumbed back the hammer, took careful aim and murmured, very faintly, barely audibly, "So long, old horse!" And then he pulled the trigger.

The bullet tore through the radiator, richocheted off the generator and then smashed into the block. Steam erupted from the radiator, and the Sears, Roebuck 10W-30 lifeblood of the faithful old Ford seeped out onto the pavement.

All of this had been visible to the sales counselor staff of the Dallas Aristocratic Motorcar Emporium, Limited, before whose Grecian temple of automotive commerce the pickup truck had gasped its last breath. It had given them all a merry chuckle, as the peasants at play so often did. The presence of the blonde, in this case, had added even zest to the event, as they searched their imaginations to explain who she was and what she was doing with the broken-down old cowboy, his Indian sidekick and that incredible old relic of a pickup truck.

"Wasn't that priceless?" one of the sales counselors said to another.

"I only wish I had my camera!" his confrere replied.

"What do you suppose they'll do now?" the first sales counselor asked.

"I have no idea," the second replied.

"Hitchhike, possibly," the first said. "Or go looking for a handout."

"My God, Wesley, you're positively telepathic!" the second replied. "Here they come!"

There were, indeed, at least two of them. The blonde was holding the arm of the broken-down old cowboy as they marched right *across* the wide expanse of putting-green-grass up to the showroom.

"He's simply ruining our lawn!" the senior sales counselor said. "I was going to slip him a couple of bucks out of the goodness of my heart, but not now!"

"I think I might be prevailed upon to assist the young lady," a third sales counselor said. The first two gave him filthy looks.

"Quick, Quincy, lock the door!" the senior sales counselor ordered. But it was too late. The broken-down old cowboy had been moving more quickly than his sort of loping had suggested. He pushed open the swinging door and held it for the blonde to step in ahead of him.

"Howdy," he said.

"Unless you've been cleared by the chamber of commerce as a worthy charitable cause," the senior sales counselor said firmly, "I'm afraid there's nothing we can do for you."

"Whuddid he say, Scarlett, honey?" the broken-down old cowboy inquired of the blonde.

"He thinks you want a handout, Uncle Hiram," Scarlett replied.

"I want to buy some wheels, neighbor," Uncle Hiram said. "My '48 Ford just gave up the ghost."

"Might I suggest that you are in the wrong place?" the senior sales counselor said. "This is the Dallas Aristocratic Motorcar Emporium, Limited, and I don't think we have what you're looking for."

"How do you know what I'm looking for?" Hiram Dalrymple asked reasonably.

"What we need is a pickup truck," Scarlett said.

"The Dallas Aristocratic Motorcar Emporium, Limited," the senior sales counselor said archly, "does not deal in pickup trucks."

"Say, J.B.," the sales counselor named Quincy said, "perhaps there *is* something."

"What do you have in mind, Quincy?" the senior sales counselor replied.

"Have you good folks ever considered going first class?" Quincy said. "What I mean to say is how do you feel about Cadillac motorcars?"

"A Cadillac pickup truck?" Scarlett asked.

"Not exactly a pickup truck," Quincy said. "More on the order of a panel truck. We just happen to have one in stock, a trade-in. It's been very well cared for and used mainly for slow trips back and forth to the country."

"You mean a hearse?" Scarlett said.

"You could put it that way, yes," the sales counselor said.

"I don't think I like you," Uncle Hiram said, expectorating to express his disapproval. A stream of brown tobacco juice flew ten feet through the air into a potted palm.

"He may have something, Uncle Hiram," Scarlett said. "Teddy Roosevelt would probably like it."

"I was so upset about losing the '48 Ford, I plumb forgot about him," Uncle Hiram said. "Okay, let's see it."

They were led to the Mechanical Maintenance Salon, or garage, of the establishment, where the senior sales counselor pulled a dusty tarpaulin off a 1951 Cadillac hearse with all the aplomb and dignity of

Hubert Humphrey unveiling a statue of Lyndon B. Johnson.

"Hardly used," he said. "A classic. They don't make them like that anymore."

"How much?" Uncle Hiram asked.

"Out of the goodness of my heart, because of the trials and tribulations I know you good people have gone through, I can make you a very attractive offer," the senior sales counselor said. "How does three hundred ninety-five dollars sound to you?"

"Not as good as two hundred ninety-five dollars," Scarlett replied.

"Sold!" the sales counselor said. "Of course, that's if you folks have a good name at the Friendly Finance Company."

"We'll pay cash," Scarlett said.

"Splendid!" the senior sales counselor said.

"Providing," Scarlett went on, "you can cut a hole in the roof so that Teddy Roosevelt'll fit in."

"So that Teddy Roosevelt will fit in?" the senior sales counselor asked.

"Teddy's my pet buffalo," Uncle Hiram replied. "Wherever I go, Teddy goes."

"Of course! There will be a slight additional fee, of course."

"Not if you want us to buy it," Scarlett said.

"You drive a hard bargain, little lady," the senior sales counselor said.

"And you will, of course, throw in a tank of gas, right?"

"My pleasure!"

"You bring any money, Uncle Hiram?" Scarlett said.

"Gee, Scarlett, honey," Uncle Hiram said, "I don't actually know if I did. Didn't figger I'd need any."

The senior sales counselor's face fell, and then his

look turned to one of curiosity as Uncle Hiram stood first on one boot and then on the other, as if he was feeling for something inside.

"Got my mad money," Uncle Hiram said. "Never know when a man's gonna need a couple of dollars." He sat down on the floor of the Mechanical Maintenance Salon and pulled off his right boot. He burrowed his hand into the boot, coming out with a small green wad.

"I don't rightly know how much I got here," Uncle Hiram said as he started to unfold the wad.

"I'll give them a check, Uncle Hiram," Scarlett said. "You can pay me later."

"Why don't we see how much he has?" the senior sales counselor said. "Perhaps it will be enough for a down payment."

Uncle Hiram separated the bills. There were four of them. He handed one to the senior sales counselor.

"Can you change a five?" Uncle Hiram asked.

"We'll have to have at least one-third down," the senior sales counselor said, taking the bill.

"Take the whole thing out of there," Uncle Hiram said. The senior sales counselor looked at the bill, and then looked at it again. There were two zeros after the fives on each corner, and then, for those with little experience with that variety of promissory notes from the Federal Reserve System, it was spelled out: FIVE HUNDRED DOLLARS. "That's the smallest I got," Uncle Hiram said. "There ain't all that much room in the toe of my boot to carry little bills."

"Lester!" the senior sales counselor called to the supervisory executive in charge of the Mechanical Maintenance Salon. "Drop whatever you're doing, and start cutting a hole in the roof of the hearse for these good people!" He turned to Scarlett. "I don't suppose I could interest you in a lovely Eldorado, could I?"

"No, you couldn't," Scarlett replied. "Daddy gave me a matched pair for my birthday. But thank you so much for your interest."

"You go get Sitting Buffalo and Teddy Roosevelt, Scarlett, honey," Uncle Hiram said. "I'll just watch this Lester fellow cut the roof off. Nothing personal, but he doesn't look like the type to be any good with a cutting torch."

Chapter Nine

It was Senior Agent C. Bromwell Fosdick's first time out as the Secret Service's agent in charge of protecting a foreign chief of state, and he was determined to see that nothing went wrong.

Just as soon as he got the word, he requisitioned, in the name of the White House, a U.S. Air Force transport plane to ferry his force of special agents to Spruce Harbor International Airport, and he had a company of paratroops flown up from Fort Bragg to establish a perimeter defense.

He had hoped to enlist the aid and assistance of the local law enforcement authorities headed by Spruce Harbor Chief of Police Ernie Kelly, but that solicitation of intergovernmental cooperation had been rather disappointing.

"If you think I'm going to send my men out to the airport at midnight, on overtime, to watch Abdullah get off an airplane . . ."

"His Royal Highness Sheikh Abdullah ben Abzug, *please,* Chief Kelly, *if* you don't mind. We must *all* be prepared to take that extra step to stay on the right side of our Arabic friends and allies, you know."

"As I was saying," the chief went on, "to watch Abdullah get off an airplane, you're even dumber than you look."

"As a patriotic American, it is your duty to do everything in your power to protect a friendly foreign chief of state from all enemies," Mr. Fosdick pressed on.

"Abdullah doesn't have an enemy within miles," the chief replied, "especially not after he sent the Blessed Virgin Mary Parochial High School all them Arab suits and the two camels for the band."

"Something has apparently been omitted from my background intelligence briefing," Fosdick said. "I wasn't aware that His Royal Highness had been here before."

"Sure, he's been here before."

"Well, since he was so kind as to outfit the parochial school band . . ."

"Not only us Blessed Virgin Mary graduates are grateful," the chief went on, "but the Protestants, too. He sent two M60A4 tanks over to Spruce Harbor High for the junior R.O.T.C. to practice on."

"As I was saying, since he has been so generous to the citizens of your quaint little dorf, don't you think it would be nice if you dispatched a force of Spurce Harbor's finest to the airport to meet him?"

"Abdullah knows he's liked around here," Chief Kelly replied. "There ain't a saloon in town that would take his money for a drink."

"A saloon in town?" Fosdick, somewhat confused, inquired. "We are talking about the same man, Chief, are we not?" He produced an 8-by-10-inch photograph and laid it on Chief Kelly's desk. It showed His Royal Higness in the Élysée Palace in Paris, France, sitting between the President of France and his wife. His Royal Highness seemed to be leering at the lady.

"That's ol' Abdullah, all right," Chief Kelly said. "He told me about her. Said her name was Françoise." He winked at Mr. Fosdick.

Senior Agent Fosdick snatched the picture back.

"May I, in any case, have your assurance, Chief, that, in the event of any untoward emergency happenstance, I may feel free to call upon you and your men?"

"That would depend on precisely what kind of an untoward emergency happenstance it happenstanced to be," Chief Kelly said. "If there was another riot or something, sure."

"*Another* riot?" Fosdick said. "Tell me about the first one."

"Nothing much," Chief Kelly replied. "Ol' Abdullah was giving a little talk to the Spruce Harbor Rotary. They have a breakfast meeting every Tuesday morning at the Spruce Harbor Holiday Inn."

"And the riot?"

"Well, ol' Abdullah carries a little bag tied to those gold ropes around that bathrobe he wears."

"We of the federal law enforcement establishment like to think of that garment as the royal robes, Chief Kelly," Mr. Fosdick said.

"Well, anyway," Chief Kelly went on, "when ol' Abdullah finished his little talk and tried to sit down, the little bag caught in the microphone and got torn loose. All the diamonds and rubies and stuff like that he had in the bag went all over the floor. It was a hell of a mess, with practically every Rotarian down on his hands and knees fighting over the jewels."

"How unseemly!"

"You said it!" the chief agreed. "I had to let the mayor have it with my blackjack to make him turn loose a ruby I got to first."

"And wasn't His Royal Highness offended?"

"Not at all," Chief Kelly said. "Whenever the

fighting seemed to die down, ol' Abdullah got some more jewels from one of his bodyguards and threw them out on the floor. It lasted about half an hour, all told."

"Well, Chief," Senior Agent C. Bromwell Fosdick said, "thank you for your time."

At ten minutes to midnight (or, as Senior Agent Fosdick thought of it, at 23:50 hours, or M-minute minus 10 of H-hour of D-day) an ambulance bearing the legend SPRUCE HARBOR MEDICAL CENTER showed up at the airport. It was, of course, stopped by the paratroops, who reported its unauthorized presence through channels to Mr. Fosdick, who had set up his command post in the control tower.

He was nearly sick at stomach with the realization that he had made a real boo-boo; he had not arranged for emergency medical facilities.

"Pass the amublance into the top-security area immediately," he ordered over the radio, and, telling the control tower operator he would be right back, he slid down the knotted rope to the ground.

The ambulance was driven by a nurse, complete to stiffly starched white hat and navy blue nurse's cape lined in red. Two disreputable-looking characters rode with her in the front seat, and two uniformed attendants were in the back.

"I'm very glad you're here," Fosdick said to the nurse. "There apparently has been a slipup somewhere in the game plan for His Royal Highness' arrival."

"Who the hell are you?" the nurse asked.

"Senior Agent C. Bromwell Fosdick, ma'am," he said, "United States Secret Service." He showed her his credentials. "I suppose it's too late to secure the services of a physician at this late hour."

"That would depend on what services you required of the physician," one of the two disreputable-looking characters said. They were both wearing sweatshirts

with MURDER 'EM, SAINTS! legends; the taller of the
two carried a medium-sized bass drum, and the slightly
shorter one carried a freon-gas-powered air horn of
the type used both by small-boat owners and football
fans.

"Open your mouth and say 'Ah,'" the one with
the air horn said.

"You're not a doctor?" Fosdick asked incredulously.

"Trapper John McIntyre," the one with the small
bass drum said, and then he gave the drum two booms.
"Co-proprietor of the Finest Kind Fish Market and
Medical Clinic, at your service."

"Providing it doesn't interfere with our departure,"
the other said.

"I naturally presumed," Fosdick said, addressing
the nurse, "because of your attire, madam, and the
ambulance, that you were here professionally."

"I had the four-to-midnight trick at the hospital,"
the nurse said, "which explains my uniform. But I
am not here, sir, professionally. If your sniffer was
working, you'd know that."

"I beg your pardon?"

"A dedicated practitioner of the nursing arts, such
as myself, never drinks on duty," Esther Flanagan
said, reaching into the pocket of her nurse's cape
and coming up with a silver flask on which was
engraved the fouled anchor with the superimposed
caduceus of the Nurse Corps, U.S. Navy. "How
about a little belt, pal?"

The sound of jet engines suddenly filled the air, and
far out over the mud flats a landing light on an air
craft suddenly turned on.

"Oh, my!" Senior Agent Fosdick said. "That doesn't
sound like a 747." He turned around and screamed
up at the control tower. "You, there! Control tower
man!"

The control tower operator, one Wrong Way Napolitano, leaned over the edge of the platform.

"Yeah?"

"Is that the Boeing 747 carrying His Royal Highness?" he asked.

"That's a Sabreliner," Wrong Way explained helpfully. "A 747's a little bigger."

"Well, you get right on the radio and tell him he can't land!"

"What did you say?"

"I said tell that little airplane he can't land here."

"You'll have to wait until that little airplane lands!" Wrong Way shouted down. "I can't hear you with all the noise he's making!"

After stamping his foot in pique, Senior Agent Fosdick started to climb back up the knotted rope to the control tower.

He made it without a good deal of energy left over, then stood wheezing and panting on the control tower balcony as the Sabreliner landed and taxied over to the control tower.

"Tell that pilot to taxi that plane to a remote corner of the field!" he shouted at Wrong Way.

"This field's got only two corners," Wrong Way replied. "Both of 'em is remote. Besides, he's already here."

He was, indeed. The plane rolled to a stop. A set of stairs unfolded from the fuselage and a tall bearded man stepped out. He was wearing denim cut-offs and a purple sweatshirt bearing the legend SURFERS DO IT STANDING UP!*

---

* Readers with good memories will recall that Flight Engineer J. Ernest "Ernie" McCluhan had told Colonel de la Chevaux that he had been surfing in Hawaii and that he didn't have much with him in the way of clothing for His Royal Highness Sheikh Abdullah ben Abzug, Sheikh of Sheikhs, *etc., etc.* Ernie wasn't kidding.

"Just look at that crazy person!" Senior Agent Fosdick sniffed to Wrong Way Napolitano.

"Sainted Chancre Mechanic!" the bearded man shouted, running down the stairs and over to the chap with the freon-gas-powered air horn. He embraced him, kissed him wetly on both cheeks, embraced him again and finally set him down.

"Your mother wears army shoes!" he boomed at the nurse, who didn't seem at all upset about the greeting, and, in fact, offered him a swig of the contents of her sterling silver flask, which he accepted readily just as soon as he had set the other weirdo, the one with the bass drum, back on *his* feet

Finally, in response to a comment from another man in the doorway of the Sabreliner, the bearded man looked up at the control tower. He cupped his hands to his mouth. "Up yours, Wrong Way!" he boomed.

"Same to you, Abe!" Wrong Way Napolitano, with a warm smile and a broad wave, called back.

"Outrageous!" Senior Agent Fosdick snorted. "Shameful! Despicable!"

He turned to Wrong Way to order him to order the pilot of the offending aircraft to be gone. It wasn't necessary.

"Spruce Harbor, Chevaux Petroleum Seventeen ready for takeoff," the radio said.

"Spruce Harbor clears Chevaux Petroleum Seventeen as number one to take off," Wrong Way replied. "The altimeter is Two-niner-niner. The winds are from the North at five. The time is . . . I'll be damned . . . zero-zero-zero-zero hours.* How 'bout that!"

"Chevaux Petroleum Seventeen rolling," the pilot reported. *"Sayonara,* Wrong Way!"

---

* It was, in other words, exactly midnight.

Mr. C. Bromwell Fosdick watched until the Sabre liner had broken ground and then disappeared into the starry sky over the rockbound coast, deeply worried until it became apparent that the aircraft, and its awful cargo, would at the last minute discover some mechanical problem that would necessitate returning to the airport, thereby reopening the awful possibility of their being seen by His Royal Highness when His Royal Highness, due right now, arrived.

"Thank God! They're gone!" Fosdick said. "My entire career as agent in charge of protecting a foreign chief of state was hanging in the balance."

Wrong Way said nothing.

"Please give me the latest report vis-à-vis the arrival of His Royal Highness," C. Bromwell Fosdick said, getting back to duty.

"You mean Abdullah? *That* royal highness?" Wrong Way replied.

"How many royal highnesses do you get here in your dinky little airport?" Fosdick sniffed.

"Well, we got Abdullah," Wrong Way replied. "And then there's Hassan. He's a crown prince, but they call him His Royal Highness, too. And then there's Woody. He's got that royal blood, too, even if he is only a duke."* He paused thoughtfully as Mr. Fosdick looked at him in shock, then went on. "And Woody's Aunt Florabelle—she's a dowager duchess."

"I am referring to His Royal Highness Sheikh Abdullah ben Abzug, Sheikh of Sheikhs . . ."

"And then there's Angus," Wrong Way plunged on,

---

* Mr. Napolitano here referred to Midshipman His Grace Hugh Percival Woodburn-Haverstraw, Royal Navy, the Duke of Folkestone and has paternal aunt, Her Grace Florabelle MacKenzie, Dowager Duchess of Folkestone. Readers burning with an insatiable curiosity to learn what these headliners of *Burke's Peerage* were doing in Spruce Harbor, Maine, consorting with the commoners, are directed to *M*A*S*H Goes to London* (Pocket Books), which, as their contribution to the 200th anniversary of rebellion in the American colonies, the publishers have seen fit to offer for sale on the better class of paperback racks.

"Florabelle's husband. He's a consort. I don't know if that makes him a royal highness or not, but he's a fine fella, I'll tell you that."

"If you don't tell me when His Royal Highness Sheikh Abdullah ben Abzug is due to arrive," Mr. Fosdick snapped, "I'll turn you over to the I.R.S.!"

"He's been and went," Wrong Way replied. "Where was you?"

"Are you trying to tell me in that barely comprehensible, if admittedly quaint, patois of yours that His Royal Highness has been here?"

Wrong Way nodded his Roman head.

"Impossible!"

"Remember the guy in the 'Surfers Do It Standing Up!' sweatshirt?"

"What about him?"

"That was ol' Abe. I call Abdullah 'ol' Abe,'" he explained. "And ol' Abe calls me 'Wrong Way.'"

C. Bromwell Fosdick's face turned ashen. He snatched his official identifying photograph of H.R.H. Sheikh Abdullah ben Abzug from his special agent's attaché case and looked at it. There was no question about it: the same hawk-like eyes; the same high cheekbones; the same white beard; the same two-carat diamond embedded in the left incisor tooth.

He picked up his official special agent's electric megaphone and stepped to the edge of the control tower.

"Attention, everybody!" he said, his voice amplified a hundredfold. "This is your agent in charge speaking! There has been a little tiny mix-up. Everybody back on the plane!"

Then he slid down the knotted rope and ran, somewhat ungracefully, toward the U.S. Air Force jet.

At about this hour, a somewhat flabby, hair-covered arm emerged from the head hole of one of the steam cabinets in the Steam and Sauna Room of the Congressional Breakfast Prayer Meeting Club, Incorporated, on Northwest K Street in our nation's capital. It waved back and forth until it caught the attention of the attendant, who rushed over, opened the latches, held the door open so that a lobster-red solon could step out and then handed the lobster-red solon a towel in which he wrapped himself.

"And how was the steam, Congressman Bambino?" the attendant asked.

"The steam was all right," Tiny Tony Bambino replied. "But I think it's outrageous that the House Committee still hasn't got The Short and Stylishly Stout model installed. It's really no fun sitting in there in the dark."

"I'm sure they're doing the best they can."

"Their best is obviously not good enough," Congressman Bambino snorted, then marched across the room to a massage table. "Where are the disinterested bipartisan witnesses?" he demanded.

"Over here, Mr. Bambino," the attendant said, indicating two respectable-looking gentlemen in terry cloth bathrobes sitting against the wall.

"In that case, you may proceed," Congressman Bambino said. "An ounce of prevention is worth a pound of cure, as I was saying to the President just the other day.* And get me a telephone, will you?"

---

* Following some scurrilous allegations by yellow journalists whose sole purpose was to discredit the Congress in the eyes of the public concerning some hanky-panky between certain congressmen and certain practitioners of the Massagic Art, the Congressional Breakfast Prayer Meeting Club, Incorporated, House Committee had authorized the employment of suitable disinterested bipartisan witnesses for their steam room. But then Congressman Edward "Smiling Jack" Jackson (Farmer, Free-Silver, Ark.) had offered an amendment. Since the function of the disinterested, bipartisan witnesses was obviously to protect the good name of Congress and its members, there was no reason why they (the congressmen) should pay for them personally with their own money. Six members of the capital police force were ordered to show up in their bathrobes at the steam room first thing the next morning.

One of the disinterested bipartisan massage witnesses was kind enough to dial a number for Congressman Bambino as he laid, somewhat unevenly, on his stomach and rocked back and forth under the ministrations of the masseuse.

"Congressman Vishnefsky is on the line, Congressman," the witness said and handed him the phone.

"Val?" Congressman Bambino said. "Tony, here. How's every little thing? The wife and all the little Vishnefskys?"

"Get to the point, Tony, I'm a busy man," Vibrato Val Vishnefsky boomed. "Cut the baloney."

"I was sitting inside the steam cabinet just now," Tiny Tony said, "to get to the bottom line."

"You mean they still haven't installed The Short and Stylishly Stout model for you yet?"

"No, they haven't, and I'm going to raise hell about it at the next prayer meeting," Tiny Tony said. "But let me get to the point."

"By all means," Vibrato Val said.

"As I was saying, I was sitting inside the steam cabinet and thinking . . . there's not even a lousy light in there . . . when it occurred to me that in addition to being Vice-Chairman of the House Committee on Honesty in Government, I am also Chairman of the Sub-Committee on Honesty in Football, Baseball and Other All-American Sports."

"So what?" Vibrato Val replied somewhat impatiently.

"It has come to my attention, Congressman," Tiny Tony said, "that certain allegations have been made, by certain responsible citizens, that one of the causes of violence in the streets among our young is the violence they see on their television screens while watching professional football."

"Tony," Vibrato Val replied tiredly, "it's after midnight. I need my sleep."

"Let me continue," Tiny Tony said. "These same responsible citizens allege that the greatest violence of all occurs when the New Orleans Saints play the Dallas Cowboys. They also allege, and I fear their suspicions are justified, that wagers are made, in violation of the law, on the outcome of the game."

"In words of one syllable, Tony, so what the hell?"

"The aforementioned teams are going to play together tomorrow, or later today, actually, seeing that I can tell by my steamproof electronic watch that it is past the hour of midnight, and thus tomorrow has become, in effect, today."

"How much Chianti did you take into the steam cabinet with you, Tony?"

"Dallas, Texas," Tiny Tony went on, "by the most innocent of coincidences, happens to be in the same great state as our dry oil wells."

"I'm beginning to see the drift of your thought, Congressman," Vibrato Val said. "Pray, continue."

"As you well know, Congressman," Tiny Tony said, "I am prepared to make any sacrifice, pay any price . . . with the taxpayers' money, of course . . . to meet my responsibilities to the fine people who have seen fit to reelect me to office."

"Me, too," Vibrato Val said.

"I am prepared, in other words, to go to Texas and see about this violence and gambling for myself."

"That's very noble of you, Congressman," Vibrato Val said.

"I know. Now, what I have in mind, Congressman, is the notion that you might similarly be disposed to tear yourself away from home and hearth and accompany me."

"I was thinking along those lines myself," Vibrato

Val said. "How far is Texas Stadium from our oil wells?"

"I don't know. But that's no problem, as I see it. When I call the Defense Department for the air force plane to take us to Texas, I'll tell them to have an army helicopter standing by in Texas."

"What about our esteemed colleague, the distinguished gentleman from Texas, 'Dry Hole' Jones? Are we going to take him with us?" Vibrato Val asked.

"Of course we are," Tiny Tony replied. "It would be a violation of congressional courtesy, even to a lousy freshman, to visit his district without taking him along. Besides, he can show us our oil wells."

"While you call the Defense Department, just to do my part, I'll call Alamo and tell him to pack his saddlebags. We're off to his home where the buffaloes roam," Vibrato Val said, jocularly, "and the bears and the billy goats play."

"That's deer and antelope, Val," Tiny Tony said, "*deer* and antelope."

"Whatever," Vibrato Val said. "Well, Congressman Bambino, see you on the Congressional Air Force Base Bus* in the morning."

---

* The Congressional Air Force Base Bus ferries members of Congress from their offices and homes to and from Bolling Air Force Base, where the air force maintains a fleet of aircraft solely to carry senior governmental officials wherever in the world their official duties require them to go. The bus was formerly a limousine, until certain yellow journalists brought the arrangement to the public's attention, and Congress unanimously forbade the use of limousines for such purposes. The vehicles currently in use, equipped with flashing lights and sirens, are Cadillac Model-75 seven-passenger motor vehicles, with a separate compartment for the driver, and on the door of which is printed, in letters a full three-quarters of an inch high, the legend CONGRESSIONAL BUS.

Chapter Ten

For most of her life, truth to tell, Margaret Houlihan Wachauf Wilson, R.N., had not had many close friends of the same gender. Once she had crossed, so to speak, the threshold between innocent childhood and the first blush of feminine maturity—when she had, in other words, begun to blossom forth above the waist and below the chin with the most visible anatomical characteristics of her sex—the other girls had immediately become violently jealous.

She had, in her high school years, been cruelly referred to by her female peer group as "Big Boobs Houlihan," and this had seemed to throw her, so to speak, into the arms of her male peer group, who, although they were quite as aware of her glandular development as the girls, had too much sense to comment upon same, at least in Margaret's company, for even then she had a well-deserved reputation for a wicked right hook.

Once she had completed her preparatory and nursing education and accepted the commission from the President of the United States to go forth and do good as First Lieutenant, U.S. Army Nurse Corps, the references by members of her peer group to her mammary gland development had been replaced by an appellation that cannot be printed in a morally uplifting time such as this.*

While she enjoyed her military career (she was ultimately retired in the rank of Lieutenant Colonel), she had not made any lasting friendships with her fellow female officers, all of whom seemed to resent the attention Nurse Houlihan was paid by her fellow officers of the male persuasion, as well as her devoted (some said "fanatic") dedication to military courtesy and protocol.

It was only after she had been retired and twice widowed that "Hot Lips" Houlihan, to use the affectionate pet name she had acquired as chief nurse of the 4077th MASH in the Korean War, finally found a pal.

This was, of course, Esther Flanagan, R.N., who had been off doing good with the U. S. Navy Nurse Corps while Hot Lips had been off with the U. S. Army, and who, by a fortuitous coincidence, had found employment in her native Spruce Harbor, Maine, as Chief of Nursing Services and head operating room nurse of the Spruce Harbor Medical Center.

Spruce Harbor Medical Center's Chief of Surgery Benjamin Franklin "Hawkeye" Pierce, M.D., F.A.C.S., and his assistant, John Francis Xavier "Trapper John" McIntyre, M.D., F.A.C.S., had also served, in the same roles, at the 4077th MASH during the period

* The reference, more commonly applied to male officers who display an unusual fervor to strictly enforce each and every petty military regulation, makes vulgar reference to the product of the excretory function of the chicken.

when Major Houlihan had been with that famous military medical facility.

It was at the 4077th MASH (known affectionately as the "Ol' Double Natural"), too, that Hot Lips had made her first true friend of the opposite gender, Boris Alexandrovich Korsky-Rimsakov, the world's greatest opera singer. The Maestro was then doing his military service under the *nom de guerre* of "Bob Alexander" and had been brought to the Ol' Double Natural leaking in several places from wounds suffered carrying his platoon sergeant, Technical Sergeant Jean-Pierre "Horsey" de la Chevaux, down a rocky Korean mountain.

Major Houlihan had been making her rounds of the surgical recovery ward tent when P.F.C. Alexander called out plaintively to her, asking if he could speak with her privately. Normally, aware as she was that when men, even men with both arms and legs encased in casts, as was P.F.C. Alexander, wished to "speak" with her, they wished to do so in what has become known as "body language," Major Houlihan would have told him to go "through channels" bringing whatever it was that he wished to discuss to be brought to her attention via one of the junior nurses. But there was something about this soldier that was different, so she violated her own rules about keeping the enlisted men in their proper place.

"What is it, soldier?" she asked.

"As I understand the purpose of this olive-drab charnel house," P.F.C. Alexander said, "it is to restore soldiers such as I to such physical condition as will make it possible for them to resume their front-line duties. Would you consider that, sir, a fair statement of the purpose?"

She bit off the reply ("Soldier, don't say 'sir' to female officers") that sprang to her lips. Her curiosity was piqued.

"That's it," she said. "What's your problem?"

"Unless you can keep your nurses away from me, lady," P.F.C. Alexander rushed on, "I'll be eligible for twenty-year retirement before I get my strength back."

"What are you suggesting?" she asked, anger and disbelief mingled in her voice.

"What you think I'm suggesting," he replied, "except that I'm not suggesting it—I'm announcing it. And wrapped up in thirty pounds of plaster of Paris like this, there is absolutely nothing I can do to escape their unwanted attention. God knows I've tried! But here I am, a trapped mouse, so to speak, to be toyed with until all my strength is gone, satisfying their lewd desires, and then cast aside like a broken toy."

She looked at him, composing the succinct little speech that would really shut him up, when she saw tears running down his cheeks.

"Why are you crying?"

"You have no idea how terrible it is to be regarded as nothing but a sexual plaything," he sobbed, "incessantly pursued by the opposite sex, with only one thing on their minds!"

"Oh, but I do!" Major Houlihan said. "I do!"

"You do?" he asked, then looked at her more closely. "Yeah, I can see why, now that you mention it."

"Put your mind at rest, soldier," Major Houlihan said. "I'll have a word with my nurses. Never again will one steal into your tent for lewd and/or lascivious purposes."

"We don't really have to go *that* far," P.F.C. Alexander said. "Maybe you could set up some kind of a roster. I realize that someone like myself has an obligation to spread as much pleasure around as possible. But this, you could say, was expecting too much of a good thing."

Major Houlihan had looked down at him, shocked to the tips of her toes with the realization that, without being all that conscious of it, her maternal instinct had compelled her to gather the weeping soldier to her bosom, in a motherly fashion, of course. As incredibly, the soldier's reaction to the proximity of her bosoms was absolutely nil.

"Say, Major," he said, wholly oblivious to the feminine charms that had driven every other male of her acquaintance, in such circumstances, bananas, "you wouldn't happen to have a little belt of something around, would you? It's been a long dry spell."

"Liquor in the wards is absolutely against regulations!" she said automatically.

"Yeah, I know," P.F.C. Alexander said. "But we understand each other, don't we? Drawn together by our irresistible, to other people, charms."

"Perhaps," she said. "A little brandy would be medically indicated to help you sleep—especially after all you've gone through, you poor lamb."

"Shake, Major," P.F.C. Alexander said. "You're all right. What did you say your name was?"

"I'm Major Margaret Houlihan," she said, "U.S. Army Nurse Corps, soldier." But then she softened. "But you can call me . . . when there's no one around, of course . . . Hot Lips."

Years later the musical world was shocked when Boris Alexandrovich Korsky-Rimsakov, the world's greatest opera singer, flew into New Orleans from Paris by chartered jet to sing at the wedding of Margaret Houlihan Wachauf* and the Reverend Buck Wilson,

---

* The bride had been previously briefly married to, and widowed by, Mr. Isadore Wachauf, Chairman of the Board of Wachauf Metal Recycling, International (formerly Izzy's Junkyard). The details of her marriages may be found in *M*A*S*H Goes to New Orleans* (Pocket Books).

announcing that he was waiving his customary fee of fifty dollars per note of music as a small gesture of affection for the lady he described as "my old army buddy."

And the Maestro was at her side, too, when the Reverend Wilson, "Blessed Brother Buck," was summoned to that final roll call up yonder.* He stood by her side when Blessed Brother Buck was planted, and it was Boris Alexandrovich Korsky-Rimsakov who urged her to accept the awesome responsibility urged upon her by the founding disciples of the God Is Love in All Forms Christian Church, Inc. After some machinations, which are far too complicated to relate here (suffice it to say they would have turned the Borgias green with envy, machination-wise), the founding disciples came to the widow Wilson to ask her to assume the leadership of the God Is Love in All Forms Christian Church, Inc., now that Blessed Brother Buck had gone to his last reward.

They wanted her, specifically, to accept ordination as the Reverend Mother Emeritus of the body, to serve, so to speak, as its symbolic mother, temporally and spiritually.

"I don't really know what to do, Boris," the widow Wilson confided, tearfully, in the man she described as her "one bosom buddy."

"What the hell, Hot Lips?" Boris advised. "Why not? Somebody's got to keep that collection of perfumed pansies in line, and you can bet your ass there's a beautiful tax dodge somewhere in that outfit."

Several years after that, by which time she had become something of a legend in New Orleans as the leader of the GILIAFCC, Inc., she learned that the Maestro had been grievously maimed in a fishing ex-

---

* The Reverend Wilson expired on the day of his marriage, quite literally upon the nuptial couch. The coroner's report listed "heart failure, due to overexertion" as the cause of death.

pedition accident while visiting Dr. Hawkeye Pierce and Dr. Trapper John McIntyre. Realizing that, by tending to his needs in his hour of pain and travail, she could in some small way repay him for his kindness and friendship over the years, she had rushed to his side in an Aero-Jet Commander provided by his old comrade in arms, now Col. (Louisiana National Guard, retired) Jean-Pierre de la Chevaux.

As critically as her professional eye judged the surgical procedures with which the fishhook had been removed from the epidermal covering of the singer's left *gluteus maximus,* she could find nothing wrong.

"I see Hawkeye hasn't lost his touch," she said to Boris. "You can pull your pants up now."

"It wasn't Hawkeye, or Trapper John, who saved my life, Hot Lips," Boris said, doing as he was ordered. "Before they could rush to my side, a local angel of mercy, a Florence Nightingale possessed of medical skills nearly as superb as your own, took the bull by the tail, so to speak, and took the hook out."

"You don't say?" she replied rather coldly.

At that moment the door to his room opened, and a nurse in uniform marched in, bearing a tray upon which sat a towel-wrapped bottle bearing a strong resemblance to a magnum of champagne.

"Get rid of the crazy lady," she said, "and you can have some of the bubbly you've been screaming for."*

---

* Nurse Flanagan's snap judgment of Nurse Wilson as a "crazy lady" was more than likely based on Nurse Wilson's (or, rather, the Reverend Mother Emeritus') attire. She had been notified of Boris' accident while presiding over the annual GILIAFFC, Inc., Come to Jesus Revival & Gumbo Boil in New Orleans' Jackson Square, and she had rushed to the airport still clad in her official vestments. These consisted, for a thumbnail description, of a form-fitting, somewhat translucent, chartreuse ankle-length gown, the bust line of which dipped almost to the navel. Resting between her mammary mounds was a twelve-inch-wide gold cross on which the words "Reverend" (vertically) and "Mother" and "Emeritus" (horizontally) were spelled out in diamonds and rubies, respectively. The same legend had been embroidered in sequins on the back of the purple-and-yellow cape the Reverend Mother Emeritus wore

"Who are you, calling me 'crazy lady,' you over-stuffed Irish pill-pusher?" the Reverend Mother Emeritus replied. "It's a good thing for you that I'm a reverend mother . . ."

"Girls, girls!" Boris said quickly, but not before Esther Flanagan had grabbed the bottle of champagne by the neck and raised it over her head. "We'll have none of that!"

They both looked at him.

"Hot Lips, say hello to Esther," Boris said. "Esther, say hello to Hot Lips."

"You're *really* Hot Lips Houlihan, U.S. Army Nurse Corps, retired?" Nurse Flanagan replied.

"You got it, chubby," Hot Lips answered.

"Boris has told me so much about you, Colonel," Nurse Flanagan said, putting the bottle down and putting out her hand. "Lieutenant Commander Esther Flanagan, U.S. Navy Nurse Corps, retired. Put it there, pal."

"Well, Commander," Hot Lips said, "perhaps I was a little hasty in making a judgment. Boris just showed me the splendid work you did on his tail."

"It was nothing, nothing at all," Esther Flanagan said. "I was glad to be of service."

"Don't be modest," Hot Lips said. "I've seen a lot of chewed-up tails in my day, believe you me, and when I say you did a first-class job on this one, you can take it as fact."

"How nice of you to say so," Esther Flanagan said, blushing furiously. "I like your outfit, a little . . . unusual . . . but . . . *nice*."

"One of the founding disciples ran it up for me," Hot Lips said, pleased by the compliment. "I think it's

---

loosely over her shoulders. And she was, of course, carrying her shepherd's crook (symbolic of her role as shepherdess of her flock) and wearing her chartreuse headgear, patterned after that worn by bishops of the Roman Catholic persuasion, except hers had little battery-powered bulbs that flashed out, every ten seconds, the message "God Is Love."

a little . . . well . . . drab. But, after all, it is a vestment, so to speak."

"Will you two knock off with the mutual admiration society and pop the cork?" Boris said impatiently from his prone-on-the-belly position on his bed of pain.

And thus began their friendship. It grew with the passage of time and shared experiences.

All of this has been to explain why, although it was just after six o'clock in the morning when Chevaux Petroleum Sabreliner Seventeen dropped out of the overcast and made its approach to New Orleans' Moisant Field, there was a good deal of activity at, in and around the terminal.

Hot Lips was determined to make Esther aware of the warm welcome she had to the Crescent City, generally, and to her neck of the worlds, as she thought of it, specifically.

Whatever the Reverend Mother Emeritus wanted, so to speak, around the headquarters temple of the God Is Love in All Forms Christian Church, Inc., the Reverend Mother Emeritus got. In this case what she wanted was a musical welcome, and the GILIAFCC, Inc., a cappella choir had been up since three A.M. getting outfitted in their lavender-and-gold lace robes, and riding out to the airfield, where, on the Reverend Mother Emeritus' signal, they would break out with "When Irish Eyes Are Smiling," "The Rose of Tralee," "Mother Macree" and "My Wild Irish Rose" the moment Esther appeared in the doorway of Horsey's little plane.

The choice of musical selection, of course, was obviously based on certain ethnic considerations. Despite the wishes of the federal government in the matter, to strike the blot of ethnicism from the national escutcheon once and for all time, Hot Lips had no intention of welcoming Esther *Flanagan* with, say, "The Volga Boatman," "Frère Jacques," or "Lili Marlene."

"Irish she is," Hot Lips mused. "And Irish she gets."

Once she had made that decision, it occurred to her that her co-practitioner of the healing arts, Reverend Mother Superior Bernadette of Lourdes, M.D., F.A.C.S., Chief of Staff of Gates of Heaven Hospital, was also a fellow Irish ethnic.

"Bernie, Margaret," she said once she got the lady she thought of as "the other Reverend Mother" on the horn. "Esther Flanagan's going to land at Moisant a little after six. I thought you might want to be on hand. The choir's going to sing some lilting Irish songs. And one of my disciples, who happens to own Unisex Florists, Limited, threw in the most *darling* floral display. It's a horseshoe, with the lilies dyed green, and the thing across the middle spells out 'Top of the Morning!' "

"I wouldn't miss it for the world," Reverend Mother Superior Bernadette said, wincing just a little. "I take it we're going directly from the airport into Dallas?"

"Right."

"See you there, Margaret," the Reverend Mother replied, broke the connection with her finger and instructed her personal secretary, Sister Piety, to get His Eminence the Archbishop on the lines instantly.

"Afternoon, Bernie," His Eminence said. "Now, what can be so important as to take me from the regular Friday Afternoon Upper Hierarchical Conference and Pinochle Game?"

"Esther Flanagan is arriving at six tomorrow morning at Moisant, en route to Dallas," Reverend Mother Superior Bernadette said.

"Well, give her my love, Bernie, and tell her I'm sorry I missed her."

"Hot Lips is going to meet her."

"How nice."

"With that pagan choir of hers," she added.

"Oh-oh."

"And she's coming with Horsey on one of Horsey's planes."

"Which means the Bayou Perdu Council K. of C., will also be on hand to welcome him?"

"Right. And the general idea, as I understand it, is that just as soon as the choir sings its welcome, the entire party will board one of the 747's and depart for Dallas."

"I'm glad you brought this to my attention, Bernie," His Eminence said. "I'll take it from here." He, in turn, had broken the connection with his finger and instructed his personal secretary, Sister Patience, to get His Honor the Mayor on the telephone immediately.

"Jupiter," he said, "this is your archbishop. Sit down and take out your pencil."

And as soon as His Eminence had explained the problem, His Honor the Mayor, Jupiter Landau, Esq., instructed his secretary, a Miss DuPree, to get Governor Steven Stephens on the line.

The governor, recognizing the gravity of the situation, instantly agreed to Mayor Jupiter Landau's request for mobilization of Company A and Company C, 414th Military Police Battalion, Louisiana National Guard, to augment the New Orleans and state police forces, which would be rushed to the airport.

If they started work now, there would be time enough to erect barbed wire and other barricades strong enough to keep the GILIAFCC, Inc., a cappella choir and congregation separated from the Bayou Perdu Council, K. of C., and its marching band long enough to get one or the other group onto airplanes and off toward Dallas.

"Once they break ground," the governor said, "they're Texas' problem."

"Right, Governor," the mayor said.

"You know, Jupiter, I just had another one of my brilliant inspirations," the governor went on.

"What's that, Steve?"

"Just to put the old cork in the old bottleneck . . . I mean to say, we should still have the M.P.'s out there and keep the hospitals on alert for riot victims, but as sort of an extra precaution, I'll tell you what we could do."

"What's that, Steve?"

"Get to the control tower operator, and have him divert Horsey's plane directly to Love Field in Dallas."

"But they replaced Love Field with that great big airport between Dallas and Fort Worth."

"Right," the governor said. "We send Horsey to Love Field, and then we arrange to have either the God Is Love group, or the Knights of Columbus, to come to the big one. By the time they can find their way out of that place, the game will be over, and our problem will be solved."

"Governor, that's a brilliant idea," Jupiter Landau said.

"Of course it is," the governor replied modestly. "That's why I'm the governor and you're just a lousy mayor."

"Moisant approach control, Chevaux Petroleum Seventeen requests landing and taxi instructions," the radio crackled in the control tower.

"Moisant, approach control, this is Air Force Six-twenty-three on priority governmental mission."

"Go ahead, Air Force Six-twenty-three," the tower operator responded. "Hold one, Chevaux Seventeen."

"Moisant approach control, by the authority vested

in me, C. Bromwell Fosdick, by the secretary of state, I order you to grant us landing priority so that me and my men can be on the ground to officially welcome and protect from all enemies, foreign and domestic, His Royal Highness, Sheikh Abdullah ben Abzug."

"Roger, Air Force Six-twenty-three. You are cleared to land. Change to radio frequency 121.2 at this time."

"Air Force Six-twenty-three leaving this frequency for 121.2," the air force pilot said.

"Chevaux Seventeen, Moisant."

"Go ahead, Moisant."

"Chevaux Seventeen, you are ordered diverted to Love Field, Dallas."

"Moisant, Chevaux has passengers to debark at Moisant."

"Don't make waves, Chevaux. We have enough problems here as it is. Just go to Dallas like a good guy."

"Moisant, Chevaux Seventeen diverting to Dallas at this time."

"Moisant ground control, Air Force Six-twenty-three. We are on the ground. Request taxi instructions to where on the field arrangements have been made to disembark the passengers aboard Chevaux Petroleum Seventeen."

"Air Force Six-twenty-three, Chevaux Seventeen is not at this field, and . . ."

"Just tell us where they're supposed to be."

"Take taxiway eleven, left. Be on the lookout for barbed wire and armored personnel carriers on both sides of the taxiway."

"Thank God," said C. Bromwell Fosdick, who was riding in the cockpit of Air Force Six-twenty-three. "Someone's on the ball. Security arrangements have been made."

Chapter Eleven

"Hey, Horsey," the pilot of Chevaux Seventeen called over the intercom, "we've just been diverted to Love Field, Dallas."

"Did they say why?" Horsey inquired, lifting his eyes from the green felt table on which cards, poker chips and a small forest of bottles had been placed, and around which sat Doctors Pierce and McIntyre, Nurse Flanagan and a bearded chap in a "Surfers Do It Standing Up!" sweatshirt.

"No."

"Get on the horn to one of the 747's on the ground and see if they know what's going on," Horsey said. "It's twenty bucks to you, Abdullah."

"Your twenty, and twenty more," His Royal Highness said. "Put up or shut up, Sainted Chancre Mechanic."

"Horsey, Lou Wallace—he's flying number Thirteen

—says it's probably because both Hot Lips' pansy choir and the K. of C. Marching Band are both waiting for us."

"Gees, I forgot all about Hot Lips' pansies," Horsey said. "My mistake. I should have remembered I told her she could have a 747. Somebody down there must like us. Get back on the horn and tell Lou I said to load the K. of C. Marching Band on board and take them to that big field, the one between Dallas and Fort Worth. Then tell the pilot of the other 747 to bring Hot Lips and her pansies to Love Field."

"Gotcha," the pilot said.

"Sorry about this, Esther," Horsey said to Nurse Flanagan. "But Hot Lips'll catch up with us soon enough."

"I understand the problem, Horsey," Esther said. "I came down here to watch a football game, not to spend my vacation patching up riot victims."

"Shut up and play cards," Trapper John said.

Meanwhile, at Parking Lot B of Texas Stadium at Dallas, in the Great State of Texas:

Having finished his regular morning ritual of an even one hundred push-ups, one hundred sit-ups and one hundred deep knee bends, Bubba Jones (a.k.a. Babcock Burton IV) set out on his ritual three-mile morning run.

He was alone in the Winnebago, having dispatched Lance Fairbanks and Brucie with orders to find the cowboy and the Indian in the photographs, and not to return until they did. He had, not without difficulty, also finally gotten rid of Fern. She had been reluctant to leave, and it had been finally necessary to tell her that he, as a typical, ordinary, run-of-the-mill ex-Green Beret, liked his women to look like women, which is to say, to have them attired in skirts and blouses, not formless "lounging jumpsuits," even if the décolletage of same was open to the waist.

Once he had said this, she had, despite the hour (six *antemeridian,* or 06:00, as they said in the Berets), immediately set out to find suitable ladies' apparel, which had finally seen him left alone.

Bubba stepped outside the lavender Winnebago and did several more deep knee bends to rid his lungs of the somewhat overpowering aura of Brucie's and Lance's perfume, which permeated the Winnebago, and then, quickly judging the perimeter of the parking lot to be about three-quarters of a mile, he calculated that he would have to do four laps to complete his self-imposed regimen of three miles a day before breakfast.

He was attired in nothing but a brief pair of gym shorts and a somewhat battered pair of sneakers, plus, of course, his dog tags, which he wore for *auld lang syne*.

The first lap was uneventful, and he saw nothing of interest except for a rather interesting, one might indeed even say "classic," 1951 Cadillac hearse sort of wheezing out of the parking lot trailing a dense cloud of blue smoke.

Pity, Bubba thought. A classic machine like that should not be allowed to degenerate and deteriorate; they didn't make them like that anymore.

But as he entered lap two, thoughts of the classic hearse left his mind as he encountered a far more interesting sight, one that quickened his senses, even as he broke into a dead run to catch up with it.

A young lady of attractive dimensions was leading a magnificent buffalo on a rope down the bushes that separated Parking Lot A from Parking Lot B.

In just a matter of minutes Bubba caught up with

them. He slowed slightly, and then, when he was parallel with them, he slowed almost to a complete halt, running in place, so to speak, so that he would not lose the inarguable benefits of healthy exercise.

He flashed a smile at the young woman, and he was more than a little surprised when it wasn't answered at all, not even with the coyest signal of acknowledgment. Usually, indeed, inevitably, when he smiled at a young woman of this age bracket, he received a dazzling smile in return.

'Good morning, miss," Bubba said finally. "I can't help but admire your buffalo."

"Buzz off," Scarlett replied.

"I beg your pardon?"

"You heard me, you physical culture freak, buzz off," Scarlett said.

"Miss, I meant simply to compliment you on your splendid specimen of *Bison Americanus,*" Bubba said. "Have him long, have you?"

She didn't even reply, which sort of staggered Bubba. He looked at her closely for the first time. She was not, he realized suddenly, just one of your typical healthy young women, with all the parts tastefully arranged in the right proportion in the proper place, but as splendid an example, biologically and anatomically, of her species as the *Bison Americanus* was of his. He was so unnerved by this realization that he said so.

"You're a splendid specimen yourself," he said, "now that I think about it."

Whereupon Scarlett Jones, without letting go of Teddy Roosevelt's rope, spun suddenly on her dainty little feet and let him have first a hard little fist in the solar plexus, and then, when he had bent over, the same fist in the right eye.

"Some people," she said, "just can't take a hint."

Bubba wheezed, but no coherent sound came out.

"I'm sorry I hit you so hard," she said, "but I am up over my ears in broad-chested jocks with the brains of a horsefly."

"I don't suppose you'd be willing to believe that I came all the way from North Carolina in search of a buffalo just like yours?" Bubba finally said.

"No, but it wasn't a bad try," she said. "Now, leave me alone!"

Bubba watched her go.

And then he heard himself calling after her. "Miss," he called, "my name is Bubba Jones. If there is ever anything I can do for you, please do not hesitate to ask. I'm in the lavender Winnebago parked over there by the men's Porta-Potties."

She didn't even turn her head in acknowledgment, although Bubba thought that he could detect a slight, somewhat disdainful, twitch of her tail.

He became aware of the sound of music—trumpets, drums, violins and even, he was sure, a couple of matched harps. He was shaken with the realization of what it was.

Little Momma had told him it would come one day: "One day, Bubba," Little Momma had said, "when you least expect it, you will hear the sound of heavenly music. It will signal the end of your care-free bachelor days, the end of your damned-fool jumping out of airplanes . . . you will be in love."

He had, at that time, been of the impression that Little Momma had been hitting the booze, but he knew now that Little Momma had been right all the time. He ran after the little lady with the buffalo and soon caught up with them.

"You're really a glutton for punishment, aren't you, birdbrain?" Scarlett said to him.

"I don't quite know how to say this," Bubba said,

running in place, taking care to stay outside the reach of her right hook, "but I think I love you."

"Out of simple compassion," Scarlett said, "for someone who is either missing most of his marbles, or plastered out of his mind at six o'clock in the morning, I will give you a friendly little warning. It's a good thing for you that my Uncle Hiram and Sitting Buffalo went out to buy us some groceries for breakfast. If either of them saw you *near* me, much less *talking* like *that,* you'd be so full of bullet holes, and so full of arrows . . ."

"My intentions are entirely honorable!" Bubba protested.

"Go take a cold shower," Scarlett said, "before I sic Teddy Roosevelt on you myself!" And, with that, she nimbly leaped up on Teddy Roosevelt's back, kicked him in the ribs and galloped off. "And stay away from me!" she called over her shoulder. "Understand?!"

"I'm your slave!" Bubba shouted after her. "Yours to command!"

"A *long,* cold shower, and then some black coffee!" she called.

"Right away!" Bubba said, then ran toward the Winnebago. "And then, after I've showered and had some coffee, I'll find you again!"

"Jesus H. Christ!" Scarlett's voice floated back to him faintly from the far corner of the parking lot, it nearly being drowned out by the sound of the buffalo's hoofbeats.

At that precise moment, Air Force Six-twenty-three rolled up before the Chevaux Petroleum hangar at New Orleans' Moisant Field.

"I thought Horsey said he was in one of his own planes," the Reverend Mother Emeritus mused.

"But who else would it be?" Reverend Mother Superior Bernadette of Lourdes* asked.

The same conclusion was reached by the leader, Henry-Philippe Trudeau, of the Bayou Perdu Council, K. of C., Marching Band.

"Okay, boys," he said, raising his baton, "hit it!"

The familiar strains of "When the Saints Go Marching In" rose in the early morning, somewhat foggy, air.

"Damn those swamp rats!" Hot Lips said. "Excuse me, Bernie, but they beat us again." She turned to the GILIAFCC, Inc., a cappella choir. "Hit it!" she ordered. "And loudly! Let's hear it for old Esther!"

A hundred voices, sort of a low-pitched soprano in timbre, burst forth with the first few bars of "When Irish Eyes Are Smiling" as the door in the side of Air Force Sabreliner Six-twenty-three unfolded from the fuselage. C. Bromwell Fosdick stepped onto the top stairs as two of the founding disciples of the GILIAFCC, Inc., in full ecclesiastical vestments, advanced on him, bearing the dyed-green lily "Top of the Morning!" floral display, and followed by the Reverend Mother Emeritus in her vestments and Reverend Mother Superior Bernadette of Lourdes in hers.

"I think, perhaps," Fosdick said, "there's been a slight mix-up. I don't really think, Sisters, that those lovely flowers are for me."

"You bet your bazooka they're not for you!" the Reverend Mother Emeritus replied. "Where the hell is Esther Flanagan?"

At that precise moment, "When the Saints Go Marching In," as being rendered by the Bayou Perdu Council, K. of C., Marching Band, died in mid-note,

---

* Reverend Moher Superior Bernadette of Lourdes had not been made privy to the governor's brilliant little plan of action, an omission he would later rue, hell having, as they say, no fury like a reverend mother ignored.

and a male voice cried out "Okay, guys, on the plane! Horsey went nonstop to Dallas."

The one-hundred-voice-strong GILIAFCC, Inc., a cappella choir kept right on, of course, at least until Hot Lips requested them to cease and desist.

"Cut!" she bellowed, making the standard "cutting" motion with her hand across her throat. "When Irish Eyes Are Smiling" died a slow death. Then she turned to C. Bromwell Fosdick.

"Who the hell are you?" she asked.

"C. Bromwell Fosdick, United States Secret Service, at your service, Sister."

"That's the Reverend Mother Emeritus to you, Jack. And, to reiterate, where the hell is Esther?"

"I'm afraid, ma'am," he replied, "I have no idea to whom you refer. My business here is to protect His Royal Highness Sheikh Abdullah ben Abzug from harm by any enemies, foreign or domestic."

"Forgive me for saying so, fella," Hot Lips said, "but you protecting Abdullah is like sending a Congressman to guard the U.S. Treasury . . . an odd idea, at best."

"I put it to you, Reverend Mother Emeritus," C. Bromwell Fosdick said, "that it is your clear, patriotic duty, if, indeed, you have the knowledge, to make me aware, as the senior governmental official on the scene, of the present whereabouts of His Royal Highness."

"I'd say that he's halfway to Dallas," Hot Lips replied. She interrupted her reply to issue another order: "Okay, guys, get on the plane! Esther's probably with Horsey, which means they didn't stop here."

"Halfway to Dallas?" C. Bromwell Fosdick inquired. "But he was supposed to land here first."

"We all have our little problems," Hot Lips said as she, taking Reverend Mother Superior Bernadette's arm, ran with her across the field and clambered aboard the Chevaux Petroleum Corporation 747 carrying the Bayou Perdu Council, K. of C., Marching Band.

C. Bromwell Fosdick climbed back aboard his airplane.

"Dallas, Texas!" he ordered. "And step on it!" He grabbed a set of earphones from a hook and put them on in time to hear the control tower.

"Moisant departure control clears Chevaux Petroleum Seven as first for takeoff, and Chevaux Petroleum Thirteen as second."

Fosdick snatched the microphone: "Control, this is Fosdick of the Secret Service. I demand takeoff priority for Air Force Six-twenty-three."

"You got it, Fosdick," Moisant departure control replied immediately. "Moisant departure control clears Air Force Six-twenty-three for priority takeoff, immediately after Chevaux Petroleum Seven and Thirteen."

"Chevaux Seven rolling," the pilot of Chevaux Six announced.

"Chevaux Thirteen rolling," the pilot of Chevaux Twelve announced.

"Air Force Six-twenty-three rolling."

"Chevaux Seven and Thirteen, Air Force Six-twenty-three, Moisant departure control. I'm handing you over to Dallas approach control at this time."

"Dallas approach control, this is Chevaux Seven. Estimate Dallas in forty-five minutes. Request landing and taxi instructions for . . . wait a minute. Hey, Lou, got your ears on?"

"Go ahead, Big Bad Bird, I got your back door," the pilot of the following aircraft replied.

"Where did Horsey say I was to go with Holy Beaver Lady? I just got word she's on here, instead of where she's supposed to be."

"Ten-four, Big Bad Bird, you got both Holy Beavers. I guess you'd better go to Love, and I'll go to

Dallas-Fort Worth with the boys, to use the term loosely. Ten-four?"

"Ten-four, Back Door," the pilot of Chevaux Seven said. "Big Bad Bird going Ten-ten. Hey, Dallas approach control, you still there?"

"Ten-four, Big Bad Bird . . . I mean, go ahead, Chevaux Seven."

"Chevaux Seven, a Boeing 747 aircraft, passing over Baton Rouge Omni at two-five thousand, estimated ground speed five-niner-zero, estimated time of arrival at Dallas four-zero minutes, requests landing and taxi instructions for Love Field."

"Chevaux Thirteen, a Boeing 747 aircraft, over the Baton Rouge Omni at about two-three thousand, estimated ground speed six hundred, wants the same thing at Dallas-Fort Worth."

The pilot of Air Force Six-twenty-three turned to Mr. C. Bromwell Fosdick.

"I can follow only one of those planes at a time, Mr. Fosdick," he said. "Which should it be?"

"You ordinary people have no conception of how lonely it is here at the top," Fosdick said. "It's one momentous decision after another." He took a quarter from his pocket, flipped it in the air and caught it against his wrist. He peeked at it.

"Heads is Dallas-Fort Worth," he said.

"Dallas approach control, Air Force Six-twenty-three for landing and taxi instructions at Dallas-Fort Worth," Air Force Six-twenty-three's pilot said.

"Ten-four," Air Force Six-twenty-three replied.

"I guess you got my back door, good buddy," Chevaux Thirteen replied.

About thirty minutes later, as the clock ticks, that is to say, about six-forty in the morning, Chevaux Pe-

troleum Seventeen came in for a landing at Dallas'
Love Field.

As they taxied toward the terminal, Dr. Hawkeye
Pierce looked up from counting the money he had just
taken from his friends on the strength of a trio of sev-
ens and a fine ability to bluff and saw a Chevaux Petroleum 747 parked on the side of the field.

"What's that, Horsey?" he asked. "Did they get here
before us?"

Horsey peered out the window.

"Naw," he said. "That one's in here to pick up some
swamp buggies* for Venezuela. See 'em?"

"Yes, I do," Hawkeye said.

"I just thought of something," Horsey said. "I'm glad
you saw that, Hawkeye." He picked up the intercom
and spoke to the pilot. "Get on the horn and tell them
to knock off loading the swamp buggies," he ordered.

"Gotcha, Horsey," the pilot replied.

"If it's all the same to you, Horsey," Hawkeye said,
"I'd rather ride to Texas Stadium in a bus with the
others. Not that I don't think your swamp buggies are
the finest kind of their genre, of course . . ."

"So would I," Horsey said. "But I sent the plane
with the K. of C. buses on it to Dallas-Fort Worth. It'll
take them all day to get into Dallas from way out
there, and you know you never can get a taxi during
a Saints-Cowboys game."

"Don't be such a spoilsport," Trapper John said.

The Sabreliner taxied over to where the larger aircraft sat, and Colonel de la Chevaux requisitioned two
of the vehicles.

---

* The vehicles to which Colonel de la Chevaux referred are oil-
industry special-purpose vehicles. Equipped with enormous (ten-foot)
wheels and tires, and powered by diesel engines, they can negotiate
practically any kind of wet, swampy terrain, hence the popular name.
Dr. Pierce was familiar with the vehicle, for Colonel de la Chevaux
had presented one to Dr. Pierce's youngest child at his birth.

"That'll be enough for us, even with Hot Lips and Reverend Mother Superior Bernadette," he said.

"Oh, is Reverend Mother Doctor coming along?" Hawkeye said. "Great!"

"That's Doctor Reverend Mother, Hawkeye," Trapper John said. "Bernie's told you that and told you that."

"I never can keep it straight."

"And Hot Lips' pansies," Horsey went on, just a little smugly, "will have to get out to Texas Stadium the best way they can."

"If I didn't know you better, Horsey," Hawkeye said, "I'd get the feeling that you didn't approve of either the GILIAFCC, Inc., congregational football society or the a cappella choir."

"Not me," Horsey said innocently. "Live and let live, I always say. It's just that it throws the Saints off their game when those guys start throwing roses at them."

"If you clowns think that I'm going to let you risk my life and limb by letting you drive me around this strange town in that swamp buggy," Esther Flanagan announced, "you've got another thing coming."

"As I understand our options, you either ride in the swamp buggy, or you walk to Texas Stadium," Trapper John said. "Is that a fair appraisal of the situation, and the options available, Doctor?"

"Well-spoken, Doctor," Hawkeye said. "You have a way with words. Pity you're such a lousy cutter."

"There's one other option," Esther Flanagan said, putting her hands on the ladder that one must climb to board a swamp buggy.

"What is that?" Hawkeye asked.

"*I'll* drive," she said, then climbed up the ladder.

Colonel de la Chevaux erred, of course. The Chevaux 747 that touched down at Love Field a few

minutes later was the one carrying the Bayou Perdu
Council, K. of C., Marching Band. Hot Lips and
Bernie had climbed about that plane, and the other
747, the one carrying the GILIAFCC, Inc., a cappella
choir and congregation had gone onto the Dallas-Fort
Worth airport.

This turn of events pleased just about everybody except Hot Lips, who frankly suspected that Colonel de
la Chevaux was entirely capable of playfully sending
her God Is Love family to, for example, Nome, Alaska,
just for the hell of it.

But she was so pleased to be with Esther Flanagan,
and after Horsey personally led the Bayou Perdu
Council, K. of C., Marching Band in their "Welcome,
Esther!" rendition of "I'll Take You Home Again,
Kathleen," that she realized she didn't have it in her
heart to stay angry with him.

"I forgive you, you miserable swamp rat," she said,
kissing him on both cheeks, following which she
climbed aboard the first of the swamp buggies and took
her place beside Esther.

By the time the band had finished playing, the self-
contained cargo elevators on the plane had lowered,
one by the one, the four Greyhound-type buses in
which the Knights traveled, to the ground.

Esther Flanagan, at the wheel of swamp buggy number one, pulled on the rope actuating the air horn. A
chorus of "Onward, Christian Soldiers," played by the
air horns atop the K. of C.'s canary-yellow buses, answered, signaling their readiness to move out. With a
mighty clash of gears, the roar of powerful diesel engines and with the K. of C. band playing "The Eyes
of Texas Are Upon Us," the convoy rolled out of Love
Field bound for Texas Stadium.

Chapter Twelve

The swamp buggy and bus convoy, however, did not, sadly, get to roll very far before minor disaster struck. Specifically, as Esther turned onto the highway into town from the airfield access road, there was what the law enforcement authorities term an "unanticipated multiple interference with a pursuit operation."

Esther Flanagan, what with the roar of the swamp buggy's diesel engine, plus the music coming from the buses behind her, certainly could not be blamed for not hearing the sirens, although there is some merit to the argument that she should have seen the flashing blue lights on the police cars.

But, as she said, immediately after the collision, "How was I to know what was going on? You don't normally see a hearse running a red light at seventy-five miles an hour with the cops on its tail."

As well as the incident could later be reconstructed, Vehicle A (a 1951 Cadillac hearse), then being pursued by Vehicles B through G (current model Ford and Chevrolet sedans of the Texas Rangers and Texas Highway Patrol, all equipped with standard siren and flashing light assemblies, said assemblies operating at full volume), ran the red stop light at the intersection of Airport Boulevard and Dallas Avenue, such action constituting still another affront to the peace and dignity of the Great State of Texas.

As Vehicle A passed Airport Boulevard, Vehicle H (a 1974 "Super Swamper" model swamp buggy) entered Dallas Avenue from Airport Boulevard, and the driver of Vehicle H thereby committed an affront to the peace and dignity of the Great State of Texas by completely ignoring the flashing lights and sirens on Vehicles B through G.

Vehicle H then struck Vehicle A in the right rear side, finally coming to a halt with its left front wheel resting in that portion of Vehicle A in which the casket generally rides.

Vehicle B then struck the left side of Vehicle H between the wheels, passing under Vehicle H the full length of its hood. Vehicle C then struck Vehicle B on its rear bumper, pushing Vehicle H even farther under the swamp buggy. Vehicle D then struck Vehicle C on its rear bumper, and in a similar manner, Vehicles E through G then struck Vehicles D through F on their rear bumpers.

Although damage to vehicles involved (except Vehicle H) was severe, no personal injuries resulted. However, in the confusion that followed the collision, during which the driver of Vehicle H further affronted the peace and dignity of the Great State of Texas by referring to the various law enforcement officers present as "the dumbest collection of Keystone Cops" she "had ever seen," adding that she "had seen a lot of dumb cops," the fugitives in Vehicle A managed to escape from their hearse, and at this writing they are still at large.

No arrests were made at the time because of the circumstances, the circumstances being that the occupants of Vehicle H were accompanied by three buses full of friends, who immediately de-bused and demonstrated with law enforcement officers in a most ungentlemanly manner.

That was something of an understatement. The decision not to make any arrests was made, in fact, only after the Knights of Columbus had de-bused, disarmed the Texas Highway Patrol officers and Texas Rangers, relieved them of their pants and left them, handcuffed with their own handcuffs, making sort of a daisy chain around the wrecked hearse.

The Texas Rangers, as is well known, do not often willingly give up their guns, take off their pants and allow themselves to be handcuffed to wrecked automobiles on major traffic arteries, and neither, to a somewhat less violent degree, do the stalwarts of the Texas Highway Patrol.

The Bayou Perdu Council, K. of C., in other words, suffered a few casualties of its own during the "remonstration." Esther Flanagan, R.N., was in bus 3, and she was tending to the rather spectacular shiner suffered by Antoine Gaspair, when she began to be aware of a gentle tugging at her sleeve.

She turned to see a cowboy and an Indian.

"I always wondered what had happened to the Lone Ranger and Tonto," she said. "Keymo Sabee, you all."

"Howdy, ma'am," the cowboy said.

"Now I know who you are," Esther Flanagan said. "You're the hot-rodder in the hearse!"

"Ma'am," Hiram said, "I'm sure sorry I got you in trouble."

"Think nothing of it, pop," Esther said. "But, tell

me, aren't you a little old to be starting off on a life of crime? You look like you'd be better off in a rocking chair."

"Squaw speak with pointed tongue," Sitting Buffalo said, smiling in approval.

"I'd like to pay for the damage, ma'am," Hiram said, reaching in his pocket and taking out a thick wad of bills.*

"Save it for your old age, pop," Esther Flanagan said, "what few years you've got left."

"Haw-haw!" Sitting Buffalo said, laughing and exposing all of his gold teeth. "Fat, red-haired squaw got your number, Hiram!"

"Shut your mouth, you lousy redskin!" Hiram said furiously.

"You tell 'im, fat, red-haired squaw," Sitting Buffalo said, whereupon Esther Flanagan punched Sitting Buffalo square in the nose, setting him on his tail.

Then she marched out of the bus. Hiram looked down at Sitting Buffalo.

"Fat, red-haired squaw got a mean punch," Sitting Buffalo said admiringly, wiping the blood from his nose with the back of his hand.

"I knew you'd get me in bad trouble sooner or later, Sitting Buffalo," Hiram said. "I never did believe when I met you in jail that you were just an innocent victim of anti-Indianism. You're a drunk and disorderly troublemaker, just like the sheriff said."

---

* Hiram had stopped off at the Republic National Bank, in which he was a major stockholder (in the mistaken belief, to be sure, that he had put his money in a Republican, as opposed to Democratic, financial institution, but a major stockholder, nonetheless), to pick up what he thought of as "a little pocket money." No sooner had he received ten thousand dollars in hundreds and five hundreds when a Texas Ranger, who had staked out the bank, spoke to him.

"Hold it right there, loony!" he had said, and the chase had begun, down the broad staircase to the lower lobby, out onto the street and into the hearse and ending only when Esther Flanagan's swamp buggy had squashed the hearse to the ground like a bug.

Then he turned and started after Esther Flanagan. He got outside the bus just in time to see Esther Flanagan roll off in the swamp buggy.

"God damn!" Hiram said.

"Up yours!" a male voice said, the speaker speaking in the honest belief that he was returning a friendly greeting.

"Smile when you say that, stranger," Hiram said, moving the heel of his hand toward the Colt-.45 single-action revolver in his belt.

"Abe doesn't speak English too well," the lady with him said. "No offense."

"Yes, ma'am," Hiram said. "Ma'am, do you happen to know that red-haired lady who just roared away in the swamp buggy?"

"Why, yes, I do," the lady said. "Why do you ask?"

"She just said something to me I don't quite understand," Hiram said.

"What was that?"

"She called me 'pop,'" Hiram said. "Now, why would she call a man like me, in the prime of his life, 'pop'?"

"I really would have no idea," the lady said, "except possibly that beard you're wearing, no offense, being down to your navel, might have had something to do with it—that, and, no offense, pop, those old clothes you're wearing."

"'Clothes make the man,' ma'am? Is that what you're saying?"

"More or less," Hot Lips replied.

"What about him, then? Even in them cut-off blue jeans and that sweatshirt . . . what does that mean, by the way, 'Surfers Do It Standing Up!'? Can't they sit down on them little boards, or what?"

"As a matter of fact, sir, I was just discussing suitable apparel with Abe," Hot Lips said. "We have decided that as nice as the shorts and sweatshirt feel, we really should be looking for your nicer clothing. Isn't that right, Abdullah?"

"Your mother wears army shoes!" Abdullah replied.

"Watch your language in front of the little lady, stranger," Hiram said.

"You're a gentleman, sir," Hot Lips said. "I can tell that."

"'That red-haired dame called me 'pop,'" Hiram said. "She didn't think I was a gentleman."

"And is it important to you that she think of you as a gentleman?" Hot Lips inquired.

Hiram looked thoughtful for a long moment before finally replying: "I'll be throwed and roped if it don't," he said. "I'll be damned."

"Up yours!" Abdullah replied with the warm smile of one kindred soul to another.

"Well, then," Hot Lips said, "if I may be so bold to make a personal suggestion, why don't you come along with Abe and me and get spruced up. Don't worry about money. I happen to have the Reverend Mother Emeritus' Emergency Fund checkbook with me, and you're a worthy cause if I ever saw one."

"That's very kind of you, ma'am," Hiram said.

"Do you know of a store nearby?"

"They got a nice little general store right here in town, ma'am," Hiram said. "And since you're being so nice to me, I'll grubstake your friend to some clothes as my little treat."

"But how are we going to get a taxi?" Hot Lips asked. "We've been standing here since the wreck, and we can't get one to stop."

"Hiram Dalrymple at your service, ma'am," Hiram said. He stepped off the curb and looked for a taxicab, and when he saw one racing toward the airport he put his fingers in his mouth and whistled. When the taxi showed no indication whatever of slowing down, Hiram pulled the Colt-.45 single-action revolver from his belt, thumbed back the hammer and shot a hole in the little flag sitting atop the taxi meter.

The taxi slammed on its brakes and skidded to a stop. The driver jumped out.

"Yes, sir? Where in the wild world can I take you, sir?" he inquired.

"Downtown," Hiram said, bowing Hot Lips and Abdullah into the taxi. "And step on it!"

Fifteen minutes later the trio climbed out of the taxi in front of a large building in downtown Dallas. They marched across the sidewalk. Glass doors tripped by an electric eye opened in front of them. They stepped inside the building.

A tall gentleman in a business suit, red carnation in his lapel, intercepted them.

"Might I help you?" he sniffed. "I mean to inquire, are you in the right place?"

"Howdy," Hiram said. "Stanley around?"

"Which Stanley is that?"

"How many you got? I mean the top hand, *that* Stanley."

"Oh, I'm afraid," the man said, "that *that* Stanley, sir, would be in conference and couldn't be disturbed."

"Let's find out," Hiram said.

"Oh, I couldn't do that," the man sniffed, and then, as Hiram reached for his Colt-.45 single-action revolver, the tall gentleman reached for the telephone. "It won't take but a moment."

Hiram took the telephone.

"That you, Stan? This here's Hiram."

"How are you, Hiram? What can I do for you?"

"You know how you been on my back all these years to come in and get outfitted?" Hiram said. "Well, I decided to take the plunge. I'm here."

"Where is here, exactly?"

"Right in front of those doors that open by their-selves."

"And is there somebody who works in the store with you? If so, let me talk to him."

"For you, fella," Hiram said, handing over the phone. There was a very brief conversation between the parties, and then the chap with the carnation in his lapel bowed deeply, snatching the carnation from his lapel and handing it to Hot Lips.

"Welcome, *welcome* to Neiman-Marcus!" he said. "How may we serve you?"

"We'll start with the barber shop," Hot Lips said. "And then we'll have a look at your top-of-the-line ready-to-wear."

Meanwhile, back at Parking Lot B of Texas Stadium:

Scarlett Jones stood before the door of the lavender Winnebago with the "Gay Power" bumper sticker, and she was very close to tears in her desperation. Teddy Roosevelt's long, rather sandpapery tongue came out of his mouth and licked her hand.

Scarlett pushed the door button. She could hear, very faintly, the chimes ringing inside. They started to play "Tiptoe Through the Tulips," but before they finished the door was flung open and she found her-self facing Bubba Jones (a.k.a. Babcock Burton IV, although not to Scarlett), who was wrapped in a towel, obviously fresh from the shower, and had a cup of coffee in each hand.

"That's a weird doorbell," she said.

"Oh, do you think so?" he said. "I rather like the sound of it. The trumpets and drums and harps sound heavenly to me, just as Little Momma said they would."

"God, you really are a weirdo," Scarlett said. "But I'm desperate. Did you mean what you said about you being my slave, mine to command?"

"Every last syllable!" Bubba replied.

"Well, put your clothes on," Scarlett said, "and I'll tell you about it."

"As much as I admire your buffalo, that splendid specimen of *Bison Americanus,* I don't think he'll fit through the door. Do you suppose he would mind being tied to the bumper?"

Scarlett tied Teddy Roosevelt to the bumper while Bubba got dressed and then entered the Winnebago.

"Now, how may I be of service?" Bubba asked.

"I want you to understand that I wouldn't be here if there were anyone else to whom I could turn," she said. "In other words, don't get any funny notions that I'm in any way attracted to you because of your blond hair, blue eyes, firm white teeth and muscular chest."

"Perish the thought," Bubba said. "Nothing would give me greater pleasure than to have you love me for my inner self."

"If you say 'love' one more time, I'll sock you in the other eye," Scarlett said.

"I understand completely," Bubba said. "Now, would it be a reasonable assumption on my part, since you say that you have no one but me to turn to, that you are alone and without family in the world?"

"It would not," she said. "I have an uncle, Hiram, who loves me and whom I love. He's part of the problem . . . I mean, he's *got* the problem."

"I see," Bubba replied.

"The thing is . . . what did you say your name was?"

"Bubba," he said. "Actually, it's Babcock, but my friends, and I hope I will henceforth be able to include you in that category, call me Bubba."

"Okay, Bubba," she said. "The thing is, Bubba, that my mother sometimes is not a very nice person."

"You don't say?"

"Like right now," Scarlett said.

"You have the advantage on me, ma'am," Bubba said.

"Huh?"

"You know my name; I don't know yours."

"Scarlett Jones."

"Then you really don't trust me, do you?"

"What are you raving about now?" she asked.

"If you trusted me, you wouldn't tell me something like that," he said. "And if you don't trust me, how am I going to be able to rush to your defense?"

"Tell you something like what?" Scarlett asked.

"That your name is 'Jones,'" Bubba said. "That's very transparent. 'Jones' is a name people use when they don't want to use their own name. I do it myself."

"I knew I shouldn't have come here," Scarlett said. "I knew it!" She got up and started to leave, but before she could get to the door it opened and Lance Fairbanks, Brucie and Fern came in.

"Now, Scarlett," Bubba said, "please don't jump to any hasty conclusions. I hardly know these people."

"Bubba," Lance said somewhat breathlessly, "you're not going to believe this, but there's an enormous buffalo tied to our bumper."

"Yes, I know," Bubba said.

"He went 'baa-baa' at me," Brucie said. "I'm simply *terrified!*"

"Talk about jumping from the frying pan into the fire!" Scarlett said.

"Who are you, and what are you doing in here with my Bubba?" Fern demanded of Scarlett.

"*Your* Bubba?" Scarlett said. "He's not much, I'll

admit, but even what he is is too much for something like you."

"Who is this person, Bubba, and what is she doing in my Winnebago?" Lance Fairbanks asked.

"It's not *your* Winnebago, Lance," Brucie said, hurt. "It's *our* Winnebago, our little *pied-à-terre* on wheels."

"I'd hate to tell you what it smells like," Scarlett said.

"Sticks and stones . . ." Brucie began.

But he stopped in mid-sentence when Bubba, taking a deep breath beforehand, bellowed, "All right, *knock it off!*"

There was a moment's absolute silence, which Fern finally broke.

"Oh, Bubba," she said, "you're so masterful!"

"Shut up, Fern!" Bubba said.

"Isn't he?" Brucie said admiringly.

"One more word out of you, Brucie, and I'll feed you to the buffalo," Bubba said.

"You're not going to feed *my* buffalo anything like *that!*" Scarlett protested.

"Shut up, Scarlett!" Bubba said. Scarlett Jones hadn't been told to shut up in ten years, and she certainly was unused to being addressed that way. She opened her mouth to reply, but before the words could come out of her mouth Bubba walked to her, picked her up by the arms and set her on top of the sink. "And don't move until I tell you that you can!" he said.

"Where would you like to sit me?" Fern asked. "How about on the bed?"

"You're really a *traitor* to the cause, Fred," Lance said. "I hope you *know* that."

"Lance, I sent you out to find that wonderful old, ugly cowboy and his faithful Indian companion," Bubba said. "And I told you not to come back until you did."

"I wanted to talk to you about that, as a matter of fact, Bubba."

"What wonderful old, ugly cowboy and his faithful Indian companion?" Scarlett asked.

"*I* have the floor, *if* you don't *mind*," Lance twittered. "And as I was starting to say, before I was so *rudely* interupted, Bubba, we're not the only ones looking for them."

"Who else is looking for them?" Bubba asked.

"Every Texas Ranger in the whole state of Texas, that's who," Lance said somewhat breathlessly.

"What for?"

"It seems the old boy is a loony," Lance said. "He's as mad as the old March Hare . . . a cuckoo flown out of the nest."

Scarlett took a small photograph from her wallet and, jumping off the sink, showed it to Lance.

"Is that the man you're talking about?"

"That's him, all right," Lance said, "el crazy man and his faithful Indian companion, crazy Indian."

"That's what I came to tell you, Bubba," Scarlett said, turning to him.

"You came to tell me my wonderful old cowboy is crazy?" Bubba asked, somewhat confused.

"He is not," Scarlett said. "He's as sane . . . *saner* than you are. My mother's just saying that. I don't know why, but knowing Momma as I do, she has her reasons, and you can bet your bottom they're really and truly rotten reasons."

"And what, precisely, is your relationship to this chap whose *compos mentis,* so to speak, is apparently a matter of some disagreement?" Bubba asked.

"He's my Uncle Hiram," Scarlett said, "the only one in the family who understands me, who really cares about me."

"Your mother doesn't care for you?"

"All my mother wants from me is to be able to relive again the thrills—the cheap thrills—she got as a U.T.M.B.P.P.G."

"A what?"

"A University of Texas Marching Band Pom-Pom Girl," Scarlett said.

"But why should she want to do that?" Bubba inquired.

"It's got something to do with getting Daddy elected President," Scarlett said.

"Your father is a politician?"

"I'm afraid so," Scarlett said.

"It doesn't matter," Bubba said after considering this a moment. "I can still hear the heavenly music. I'll marry you, anyway."

"Bubba!" Fern said. "How could you, after all we've been to each other?"

"What is she talking about, Bubba?" Scarlett asked.

"I'll tell you this, miss," Brucie said, "Fern, or Fred, or whatever she calls herself, simply can't be trusted."

"We have digressed, I fear," Bubba said. "If you tell me, Scarlett, that your Uncle Hiram is sane, that's good enough for me. The problem, then, as I see it, since the Texas Rangers are after him, obviously intending to truss him up and run him off to the funny farm, is to reach him first and spirit him out of here."

"Where will we take him?"

"I have just the place," Bubba said. "My farm! I came here to talk to him, and his being at the farm will provide the opportunity to which I am denied here."

"What do you want to talk to my Uncle Hiram about?" Scarlett asked.

"Don't bother your pretty little head about it, my dear," Bubba said. "It's man-talk."

"You're a shameless, insufferable male chauvinist pig!" Scarlett said.

"And it's a good thing for you, dear Scarlett," Bubba said, "that I am."

He reached for the C.B. microphone.

"Breaker, breaker," he said. "Any old Camp Mc-Call* graduates with their ears on, come back to Pigman."

Scarlett and the others looked at him in utter confusion. But the replies came immediately.

"Go ahead, Pigman, you got 8th Special Forces Company, Texas National Guard."

"Go ahead, Pigman, you got Green Beret Post 5660, V.F.W."

"This is Pigman," Bubba said. "I'm having a little trouble with the Texas Rangers and need assistance. Physical violence may be required. Come back."

"What's your ten-twenty, Pigman?"

"Parking Lot B, Texas Stadium. The old ten-twenty's a lavender Winnebago."

"Ten-four, Pigman. This is Green Beret Post 5660, V.F.W. We came here to the Texas Stadium, Ten-twenty, to fool around with some crazy Cajuns from Louisiana, but this sounds like more fun. Hot damn, good buddy, we're on the way!"

"Pigman, this is the commanding officer of the 8th Special Forces Company, Texas National Guard. Inasmuch as we have been ordered here by our beloved governor to aid and assist the Texas State Troopers in maintaining order, we cannot, of course, come to your assistance. On the other hand, of course, we don't have to assist the Texas Rangers with a whole

* Camp McCall, North Carolina, is where the men of Special Forces, the Green Berets, receive their basic training. It is known as the "John Wayne Course."

lot of enthusiasm, either, and if our good buddies in Post 5660 can't handle the situation, give us another yell. Seventy-threes to you, good buddy. Eighth Special Forces going Ten-ten."

Chapter Thirteen

When the Honorable Alamo Jones spoke to his little Ida-Sue on the telephone to tell her that the Honorable Vibrato Val Vishnefsky had just told him he was going home to Texas with him and the Honorable Tiny Tony Bambino, Ida-Sue wasn't exactly beside herself with joy.

"Ida-Sue," Alamo said, "do you really think that an FUTMBPPG and future First Lady of our beloved nation should be using language like that?"

"Shut your fat mouth, Alamo," Ida-Sue replied. "and listen carefully. Not only haven't I been able to find Scarlett, but I can't find Uncle Hiram and his goddamned faithful Indian companion, either."

"I thought you had the Texas Rangers looking for them, Ida-Sue, and I know the Texas Rangers always get their man."

"That's the Northeast Mounted Police who always

get their man, dummy," Ida-Sue said. "The Texas Rangers get their man and then let him go."

"You mean they had poor Uncle Hiram and he got away?"

"You got it, Alamo. Slipped right through their fingers."

"Well, I'm sure they'll be able to find him again soon, Ida-Sue," Alamo Jones replied. "I mean, how many bearded old men with faithful Indian companions are running around Texas loose?"

"At last count, according to Wally . . . "

"Who's Wally, Ida-Sue? I don't believe I've had the pleasure . . . "

"Wally Dowd, the head Texas Ranger, dummy," Ida-Sue said. "At last count, Wally said his men had arrested one hundred thirty-eight bearded old men running around with Indians. Not one of them was Uncle Hiram."

"Well, I'm sure something will turn up, Ida-Sue," Alamo said soothingly.

"Yeah, like you and those two dummies are going to."

"I really don't think you should refer to members of Congress in quite those terms, Ida-Sue."

"You're right," she said. "But as a dutiful wife, I'm not using the only language that really describes them."

"What do you want me to do, Ida-Sue?"

"We can't let Vibrato Val and Tiny Tony get near the ranch, Alamo," Ida-Sue said. "Even as dumb as they are, they can tell the difference between an oil rig and no oil rig, so we'll just have to keep them busy."

"How should I do that, Ida-Sue?"

"Texas hospitality," Ida-Sue said. "Deck them out in

ten-gallon hats and cowboy boots, and get and keep them drunk."

"Good thinking, Ida-Sue," Alamo Jones said.

"One more thing, Alamo. You ever hear of Teddy Roosevelt?"

"Of course I've heard of Teddy Roosevelt!" Alamo replied. "I am, after all, a United States Congressman. Teddy Roosevelt was our beloved president all through World War II. I believe he was a Yankee. What about him? I thought he was dead."

"I mean somebody alive *now* named Teddy Roosevelt."

"Maybe he had a son or something."

"I mean somebody named Teddy Roosevelt who would be running around with Uncle Hiram and that damned Indian."

"Can't say that I do, Ida-Sue," Alamo replied after a moment's thought. "Why do you ask?"

"Wally tells me that some guy with that name plus . . . and I didn't tell you this yet . . . some blonde bimbo are with Uncle Hiram and the Indian."

"I gotta go, Ida-Sue. I can hear the horn on the congressional bus. It's playing 'The *Washington Post* March.' "

"Don't fail me, Alamo," Ida-Sue said with just a hint of menace in her voice. "Do something right for a change."

And so it came to pass that when Air Force Congressional V.I.P. flight 103, a Sabreliner, touched down at Dallas' Love Field, and the band of the 114th Quartermaster Battalion, Texas National Guard, began to play "The Eyes of Texas," two rather odd-appearing individuals fell out of the airplane and had to be assisted to their feet.

Despite the high-heeled cowboy boots with which they were shod, they managed to stay erect during the playing of what is *de facto* the Texas national anthem, with their ten-gallon hats held reverently over their hearts. It was only when the musical rendition had been concluded, and they replaced their hats, that one could say with any degree of certainty that they'd been at the sauce. Their headgear had apparently been swapped when they fell out of the airplane, for the hat that the Honorable Vibrato Val Vishnefsky placed on his flowing silver locks was obviously designed for a man with a larger head; it came down over his ears, blinding him.

"Gimme back my cowboy hat, you miserable, sawed-off spaghetti-eater," the congressman said somewhat thickly.

Congressman Tiny Tony Bambino replied, none too clearly, "That's the trouble with you lousy, pinheaded Polacks—you can't hold your booze." Then he kicked Congressman Vishnefsky in the shins with the pointed toe of his cowboy boot.

They were finally separated, but only after they had rolled around the somewhat greasy surface of the parking area, and loaded into the official limousine by four husky Texas Rangers. In the confusion, however, Congressman Alamo Jones was left behind at Love Field.

By the time the congressmen arrived at Texas Stadium, each with two large Texas Rangers on their laps, the swamp buggy-bus convoy bearing the Bayou Perdu Council, K. of C., Marching Band had already arrived (less, of course, the Reverend Mother Emeritus and His Royal Highness, Sheikh Abdullah ben Abzug, who were off shopping, but including Doctors Pierce and McIntyre, Reverend Mother Superior Bernadette of Lourdes and Sitting Buffalo).

Upon their arrival, the Bayou Perdu Council, K. of C., Marching Band had formed ranks and, to the delighted applause of football fans in the parking lot, they had marched off to their reserved seats while playing "When the Saints Go Marching In."

Horsey de la Chevaux remained behind to assure Reverend Mother Superior Bernadette of Lourdes that, although Hot Lips and Abdullah were among the missing, there was nothing to worry about. Hot Lips, in more ways than one, was a big girl.

Sitting Buffalo, who had more or less sobered up, was following Reverend Mother Superior Bernadette around like some outsized, befeathered cocker spaniel and telling her of his happy childhood under the good sisters at the reservation school, a subject in which, truth to tell, Reverend Mother Superior Bernadette was somewhat less than fascinated.

Moreover, since Sitting Buffalo persisted in referring to Esther Flanagan, R.N., as "fat, red-haired squaw," the Reverend Mother suspected that it was just a matter of time before Esther forgot that she was a retired officer and gentlewoman and gave him another belt in the snoot.

"Dr. Pierce," Reverend Mother Superior Bernadette of Lourdes said, ever so sweetly, "I would be ever so grateful if you would take Tonto, here, someplace else, even if it means that he won't be able to tell me any more about what Sister Mary Agnes taught him in school."

"Dr. Pierce?" Hawkeye inquired. "I thought we were on a first-name basis; I thought we were friends."

"Friends? Friends?" Reverend Mother Superior Bernadette inquired incredulously. "I hold you responsible for this whole affair, you lousy heathen-healer. Now, get this besotted red man out of here, and take backsliding McIntyre with you!"

Dr. Pierce took Sitting Buffalo's left arm and Dr.

McIntyre his right, and they led him off through the parking lot.

"Hey, Hawkeye," Trapper John said, "take a look at that lavender Winnebago."

"I see it, but I don't believe it," Hawkeye said.

"We go to wigwam on wheels," Sitting Buffalo announced. "I know wigwam on wheels. Wigwam on wheels has firewater in refrigerator."

"I don't think that's such a good idea, chief," Hawkeye protested, but his objections were to no avail. Dragging them behind him, Sitting Buffalo strode purposefully over to the lavender Winnebago. Teddy Roosevelt, who hadn't very much liked being left alone tied to the bumper, and who, indeed, was unaccustomed to being tied up at all, saw him and started out to meet him. The rope that held him was a strong rope, and something had to give. The Winnebago moved sideways toward Dr. Pierce, Dr. McIntyre and Sitting Buffalo, knocking a Buick, two Toyotas and a Honda 750 motorcycle out of the way, rather noisily, as it did so.

"Oh, my God!" Brucie said. "It's the end of the world!"

"What the hell?" Bubba said.

"It's your damned buffalo—that's what it is!" Fern said to Scarlett.

Scarlett ran to the door and jumped out, with Bubba right behind her.

"Teddy Roosevelt!" Scarlett shouted. "Bad boy! Come here!" Teddy Roosevelt stopped and hung his massive head. And then Scarlett saw Sitting Buffalo. "Oh, Sitting Buffalo, I'm so glad to see you!"

"How!" Sitting Buffalo said. "Firewater still in wigwam on wheels?"

"Quick, get in the Winnebago before someone sees you," Scarlett said.

"My friends," Sitting Buffalo said, indicating Drs. Pierce and McIntyre by picking them two feet off the ground one at a time.

"Bring them along," Scarlett said. Sitting Buffalo did just that.

The sound of the rending metal and breaking windshields brought Green Beret Post 5660, V.F.W., which had already been en route, on the run. It also attracted the attention of the law enforcement officers on the scene, who came running from the other direction, blowing whistles, shouting and making other police-type sounds and noises.

Dr. Pierce, whom Sitting Buffalo had placed, like a housewife placing a can of beans on her kitchen shelf, on the little ledge behind the windshield of the Winnebago, turned to Dr. McIntyre, who had been similarly installed on the engine cover.

"Trapper John," he said, speaking from vast experience in matters of this kind, "it would appear that the battle is about to be joined."

"Finest kind," Trapper John said.

A hearty cry, "Remember Fayetteville!" floated through the air.

"Last one in is a lousy paratrooper!" another stalwart in a beret called.

"What sort of green hat is that the fat chaps are wearing?" Trapper John inquired.

"That's not a hat, Trapper John," Hawkeye replied. "It's a beret. The fat fellows are obviously some sort of French affiliate of some Masonic order akin to the Tall Cedars of Lebanon or the Shrine."

"Firewater," Sitting Buffalo said, handing each of them a bottle. "Tickles the nose."

Hawkeye examined the bottle. "Oh, domestic bubbly, San Joachim Valley, '76," he said. "An amusing little wine, as I recall." He ripped off the gold foil at the neck, untwisted the wire and gave the bottle a little tap with the heel of his hand. The cork flew out with a loud pop.

"My God!" Brucie cried from where he and Lance Fairbanks huddled together under the bed. "They're shooting at us!"

Trapper John opened his bottle and turned with anticipation to witness the meeting of the opposing forces.

"I wonder what it's all about," Hawkeye inquired rhetorically.

"Never look a gift horse in the mouth, Doctor," Trapper John replied. "I'll bet you three-to-five on the fat guys in the berets. They have a certain something, a certain *je ne sais quoi,* about them."

But then something astonishing happened. At the very last moment, as the advance elements of the opposing forces warily advanced the last few feet toward one another, a whistle blew, three shorts and longs. But it was not the signal Trapper John and Hawkeye naturally assumed it to be, the signal to charge. It was quite the reverse. With obvious reluctance, but with good discipline, the law enforcement officers lowered their nightsticks, cans of Mace and blackjacks and withdrew.

Green Beret Post 5660, V.F.W., was so surprised by this tactic that they did not exploit the withdrawal. They simply stood there, fists cocked and mouths opened in surprise, as the police sort of melted away through the parked cars and then formed ranks in one of the driveways fifty yards from the front line.

What had happened was that a bulletin had come in by radio from the Texas Rangers' mobile disaster command post: "Attention, all police forces! Attention, all police forces!" the message began. "Stand by for a personal bulletin from beloved Wally Dowd himself!"

In a moment, the somewhat gravelly voice of head Texas Ranger Wallington T. Dowd himself came over the air.

"Men," he began, "this is your commanding officer, Wallington T. Dowd. I have just received word that the loony we have all been looking for has been taken into protective custody, together with one of the three persons with whom he was known to be traveling, and this despite the fact that he had cleverly disguised himself by cutting off his beard. To preclude a reoccurrence of that unfortunate incident at the Republic National Bank, during which the loony and his faithful Indian companion got away, all law enforcement officers under my command, which means everybody with a badge, are ordered to form a line around my command post. The loony shall not get away again, or my name isn't Wallington T. Dowd! That is all!"

But it wasn't quite all. Thirty seconds after that another message flashed over the airways.

"Men, this is Wallington T. Dowd again," the head Texas Ranger said. "Here is an update on my last bulletin. While we have not yet determined which of the two scoundrels we have in custody is the loony, we have determined that neither of them is that lousy Indian. Neither of them is wearing a feather, and both of them have rather pasty-looking pale faces. So continue to be on the lookout, men, for that lousy Indian and the blonde hooker! Wally Dowd, out!"

There being no police radio in the lavender Winnebago, there was, of course, no way for its occupants to become aware of what had transpired. All they knew was that the police had withdrawn, leaving behind them a very disappointed group of fat fellows in green berets.

"Cheer up, men!" one of these called to his fellows.

"Those crazy Cajuns are around here somewhere. I see their yellow buses. We'll have our little fun yet!"

At about this time a convoy of automobiles, all equipped with flashing lights and sirens, raced toward Texas Stadium from the Dallas-Fort Worth airport.

In the front seat of the first car, a somewhat ashen-faced C. Bromwell Fosdick turned to the driver, one Leonard J. Watson, who was the Secret Service agent in charge of the Dallas office.

"Lenny," he said, then was unable to go on.

"What is it, Bromwell?" he asked gently. "There should be no secrets between us of the Secret Service."

"Lenny," C. Bromwell Fosdick blurted out, "I would consider it a personal favor if you didn't tell anybody about what happened out there."

"Put your mind at rest, Bromwell," Leonard J. Watson replied. "It happens all the time."

"It does?"

"Why, only last week the mayor of Fort Worth got lost in there. They had to mobilize the whole Dallas-Fort Worth district of the Boy Scouts to go in and find him."

"Really?"

"Really," Lenny said. "He was hysterical when they finally got to him. He'd been living for three days on nothing but Dr Pepper and those little cracker-and-peanut-butter sandwiches you get out of the vending machines for a dollar."

"Don't you mean a quarter, Lenny?"

"They're a dollar at Dallas-Fort Worth," Lenny explained. "But don't worry, Bromwell, my lips are sealed. Washington will never hear about it—at least not from me."

"You're a true brother of the Secret Service, Lenny."

"Thank you, Bromwell," Lenny said. "Now, what

about our little problem with this Arab chap? There's going to be a bunch of people at Texas Stadium."

"How many Arabs are there going to be in cut-offs and sweatshirts with naughty writing on them?"

"Far be it from me to tell you how to handle your foreign dignitary, Bromwell, but I would like to offer a teensy-weensy little thought I had."

"By all means, Lenny," C. Bromwell said. "I'm always open to suggestions."

"It occurred to me, Bromwell, that if His Royal Highness changed his royal robes for cut-offs and a sweatshirt, it's within the realm of possibility that he might exchange his cut-offs and sweatshirt for some other clever disguise."

"I was thinking along the same lines myself, oddly enough," C. Bromwell Fosdick replied, but not very convincingly.

"I'm sure you were, Bromwell," Lenny said. "And what conclusion did you reach?"

"You first," Fosdick said.

"Well, if I were you, Bromwell, I wouldn't confine my efforts to searching for someone in cut-offs and a sweatshirt. I mean, you have to consider the possibility, as terrible as it is, that you might not find him. How would it look back at headquarters, in our nation's capital, if it got out that you had chased His Royal Highness from Maine to Louisiana to Texas without even catching up to him, much less protecting him from all enemies, foreign and domestic?"

"I appreciate your suggestion, Lenny," Fosdick said. "You're really a very nice chap."

"You're welcome, I'm sure," Lenny said.

Fosdick picked up the two-way radio-microphone. "Fosdick of the Secret Service speaking," he said. "A change to my bulletin 404 is announced. In the sentence that reads, 'Be on the lookout for an Arab sheikh dressed in cut-offs and a sweatshirt with naughty words on it,' delete 'in cut-offs, *et cetera*,' and substitute, therefore, 'in any kind of clothing, and who answers to the name of Abdullah.' Confirm."

"Confirm. We are to locate and protect from enemies, foreign and domestic, an Arab, answering to the name of Abdullah, who may be dressed in any kind of clothing."

"Affirmative," Fosdick replied. "Fosdick, out."

"God loves you!" a voice said, by way of answering the telephone.

"Thank God someone's there!" the caller said. "With whom do I have the pleasure of speaking?"

"This is Brother Tiffany."

"Brother Tiffany, this is Brother Lester," the caller said, "of the headquarters temple."

"And how may I be of service, Brother Lester?"

"Brother Tiffany, there's been the most awful mix-up. We've lost the Reverend Mother Emeritus."

"Isn't that odd? Just a moment or two ago I saw the Reverend Mother Emeritus rolling down Maple Avenue in the most *gorgeous* Rolls-Royce you ever saw, and she was with two divinely handsome English types."

"Well, all I know, Brother Tiffany, is that the a cappella choir and I are simply stranded here in the most lonely airport you ever saw."

"That must be Dallas-Fort Worth. Tell me, dear, is there a big statue of a cowboy in the main passenger terminal?"

"Not that I saw. All that I can see is just miles and miles of corridors."

"Well, if you were at Love Field, you couldn't miss the cowboy," Brother Tiffany said. "So you must be at

Dallas-Fort Worth. Whatever possessed you to go way out there?"

"The pilot, the one who called me a 'perfumed pansy' and who told me to stay out of the men's room, probably did it to be nasty. But that's water under the dam, Brother Tiffany. The bottom line is that here we are, and I don't even know where Texas Stadium is, much less how to get out of this awful airport."

"Well, whatever you do, Brother Lester, don't start roaming around; otherwise we'd never find you. You'd spend the rest of your life out there drinking Dr Pepper and eating cracker-and-peanut-butter sandwiches at a dollar a crack."

"I know. I put a quarter in the machine and a tape-recording laughed at me," Brother Lester said. "And then it kept the quarter."

"I'll see if I can get our bus drivers on the C.B. and have them come get you."

"Oh, thank you, Brother Tiffany."

"Think nothing of it, Brother Lester. I mean, if we in the GILIAFCC, Inc., don't care for each other, who will?"

Chapter Fourteen

"Howdy, Ida-Sue," Alamo Jones said. "This here's your husband."

"I would never have guessed," Ida-Sue replied. "Where are you, Alamo?"

"At the airport," Alamo said.

"And are Tiny Tony and Vibrato Val with you?"

"Yes and no, Ida-Sue," Alamo said.

"What the hell is that supposed to mean?"

"Well, I came with them on the plane, and I gave them the hats and the boots and all they wanted to drink . . ."

"And?"

"They're on their way out to Texas Stadium," he said. He had a sudden inspiration, based more or less on the truth. "There wasn't room for me in the car," he added.

"My God!" Ida-Sue said. "You've finally done something right."

"I have?" he asked, somewhat surprised.

"I probably shouldn't tell you this, Alamo, lest you get the idea that I'm turning into a sissy or something, but I really don't have the heart to face Uncle Hiram."

"Have they caught him?"

"I just this minute got the word that the Texas Rangers finally caught him and one of the others—not that goddamned faithful Indian companion, but the other one, Teddy Roosevelt. The hooker and the Indian are still on the loose."

"They'll catch them, I'm sure," Alamo said.

"So what I'll do, Alamo," Ida-Sue said, "is go out to the gate and greet them when they arrive. That way, I don't have to face Uncle Hiram. Fat Jack Stewing, the shrink, and Richard Crochet, the shyster, can handle the dirty business themselves."

"I'll get out there just as soon as I can, my dear," Alamo Jones said.

Hawkeye and Trapper John turned from looking through the windshield of the lavender Winnebago.

"Nice little place you've got here," Trapper John said.

"Whose nice little place, exactly, is it?" Hawkeye asked.

"His," Scarlett said, pointing at Bubba.

"Theirs," Bubba said, pointing to Lance and Brucie, who were still under the bed.

"Hi, there!" Lance called out.

"Pleased to make your acquaintance, I'm sure," Hawkeye said. "Hey, chief, how's the supply of firewater?"

"Firewater all gone," Sitting Buffalo said. "Sitting Buffalo will go get more firewater. Will get some firewater for fat, red-haired squaw, too."

"Sitting Buffalo, you can't go out there!" Scarlett

protested. It was to no avail. Brushing aside Scarlett and Bubba with absolutely no visible effort, Sitting Buffalo set out to acquire some additional firewater. The good sisters at the reservation school had taught him to read, not too well, to be sure, but well enough to recognize a Budweiser sign when he saw one.

"Men," Bubba called out to Green Beret Post 5660, V.F.W., "go with him!" Then he turned to Scarlett. "Put your mind at rest, little lady," he said. "Sitting Buffalo is as safe with the men who wear the green beret as he would be in his mother's wigwam."

"Thanks a lot," Scarlett said sarcastically.

"You're welcome, I'm sure," Bubba replied. "Now, is there anything else I can do for you, Scarlett?"

"Flake off," Scarlett replied. "No, wait a minute. I forgot all about poor old Teddy Roosevelt."

"What about poor old Teddy Roosevelt?"

"The poor lamb hasn't had anything to eat since we left the ranch," Scarlett said, "except for the rosebush he ate at the Dallas Aristocratic Motorcar Emporium, Limited."

"Put your mind at rest, little lady," Bubba began.

"If you call me 'little lady' one more time, you oversized Boy Scout . . . "

"I was an Eagle Scout, as a matter of fact," Bubba said, "as well as a junior assistant scout master."

"I'll feed *you* to Teddy Roosevelt!" Scarlett concluded.

"The *Bison Americanus* is not a carnivore," Bubba replied. "I should think you would know that. You haven't been feeding that poor beast hot dogs or anything else unhealthy like that, have you?"

"Of course not," she snapped.

"I'm relieved," Bubba said. "Generally, those of your sex are not very well versed in animal nutrition."

"What am I going to get Teddy Roosevelt to eat?" Scarlett asked.

"As I was saying just a moment ago, little lady . . . " Bubba began, and Scarlett kicked him in the shins. He winced, but otherwise pretended not to notice, and went on. " . . . as one more manifestation of my burning, if newfound, desire to not only satisfy your every little wish, but to anticipate your wishes, you may put your mind to rest. I have just the thing, I hope, for Teddy Roosevelt."

"What the hell are you talking about?" Scarlett asked.

"If you'll just watch this," Bubba said, and picked up his pack.

"What the hell is *that?*"

"It's my luggage, obviously," Bubba replied. "You mean you've never seen a Green Beret Handy-Dandy Rucksack and Marching Pack before?"

"Neither have I," Hawkeye said, "but I like it."

"I should have known you wouldn't have had something as simple as a suitcase," Scarlett said.

"One has trouble getting through airplane doors with suitcases," Bubba said. "And then the shock that follows the canopy opening has a nasty way of jerking hand-held suitcases from one's hand."

"Do you have any idea what he's talking about?" Scarlett asked Trapper John.

"I gather that he is a parachutist," Trapper John replied. "They're not like you and me, parachutists aren't."

"What is that thing?" Scarlett asked as Bubba unfolded a collapsed canvas device.

"It's a folding bucket," Bubba explained.

"And what's that awful-looking powder?" Scarlett inquired, then gagged at the smell. "If it didn't smell so bad, I'd think it was laundry detergent."

"Nasal beauty is in the nostrils of the beholder," Bubba said. "This is *Soja hispida Burtonosis*. It's dehydrated, of course, and fortified with certain minerals considered necessary for bisonal nutrition."

"Do you know what he's saying?" Scarlett asked Hawkeye.

"I think he's going to try to get your buffalo to eat that stuff," Hawkeye replied.

"Over my dead body!" Scarlett said.

Bubba ignored her. He filled the canvas bucket about a third full with the powder, and then he filled the bucket with water from the sink faucet. An even stronger odor now filled the trailer. The stuff in the bucket bubbled and fizzed, then subsided, leaving a thick brown substance.

"Yuk!" Scarlett said, holding her nose as she looked at it.

"You're not really going to let him feed that stuff to your innocent buffalo, are you?" Trapper John asked.

"I'm going to let him try," Scarlett said, "and then laugh and laugh as Teddy Roosevelt kicks him back to wherever he comes from."

"That's very cruel of you," Hawkeye said.

"He who laughs last laughs best," Bubba said, stepping to the door, "to coin a phrase."

"Been nice knowing you," Hawkeye said.

"He probably doesn't even have hospital insurance," Trapper John said. "We're going to have to put him back together for free."

Bubba opened the door. Teddy Roosevelt was standing there, snorting and making other buffalo-type noises and pawing the parking lot with his foot.

"Here you go, old fella," Bubba said. "Chow-down, as we say in the Green Berets."

He extended the bucket to Teddy Roosevelt. Teddy Roosevelt stuck his massive jaw (all that would fit of it, anyway) into the bucket. There was a rather awesome slurping sound, and then the jaw was withdrawn. The bucket had been emptied. Teddy Roosevelt looked at Bubba. His right foot rose off the ground.

"Watch out, fella!" Trapper John said. "I think he's about to kick."

"No, he's not," Scarlett said, wonder and awe in her not unpleasant voice. "He's giving Bubba his paw. I taught him how to do that. He wants more of that stuff."

"Will wonders never cease?" Hawkeye said.

"What's in that, anyway?" Trapper John asked.

"Yeah, what *are* you feeding my buffalo?" Scarlett said. "Is it good for him?"

"What you have just seen, little lady," Bubba said, "is a preview of what will be a virtual revolution in buffalo-feeding in America. It will open a whole new vista of opportunity for buffalo breeders and, coincidentally, solve a minor problem that Little Momma and I have been having."

Scarlett was so shaken that she forgot to kick Bubba for calling her "little lady." She rectified her omission by punching him in the back as he refilled the bucket for Teddy Roosevelt. When he didn't seem to notice, she punched him again, and then again.

He finally turned around. "You've got a lot of spirit, little lady," he said. "I like that in girls."

She punched him in the stomach, with no visible results at all, and then she punched him two or three more times, equally without any result. Finally, she stood there, puffing, red faced, furious.

"Ain't love grand?" Hawkeye said.

"That's what makes the world go 'round," Trapper John philosophized.

"Something wrong, little lady?" Bubba asked, seeing the confused look on Scarlett's face.

"What's that noise?" Scarlett asked. "What's that noise?"

"What noise is that?" Bubba asked.

"Trumpets, violins, and I think a couple of harps," Scarlett said. "Can't you hear it?"

"Of course I can hear it, little lady," Bubba said.

"Did I miss something?" Fern said, coming from the rear of the Winnebago and placing a feminine hand on Bubba's shoulder. "How goes it, big fella?"

"Get your ugly paws off my fiancé!" Scarlett said furiously. "You skinny old bag! I'll pull your hair out!"

When Ida-Sue Jones arrived at the V.I.P. gate at Texas Stadium, she found the passageway blocked by a Rolls-Royce. The occupants of the vehicle were a lady, in what looked like an evening gown of the type worn by proprietors of establishments with red lights in the window, and, surprisingly, two Englishmen, in dignified bankers'-gray suits, complete to derby hats and rolled umbrellas.

"Get those lousy foreigners and their hooker out of the way!" Ida-Sue screamed. "Congressman Tiny Tony Bambino and Congressman Vibrato Val Vishnefsky will be here any moment!"

Ida-Sue looked at the lousy foreigners who were interfering with her well-laid plans, and then she did a sudden double take, taking a very close look at the chap with the neatly trimmed regimental-type brush mustache.

"For your information, lady, them congressmen you mentioned already passed through," the policeman said.

"What are you waiting for, you Jackass!" Ida-Sue screamed. "Arrest him!"

"Beg pardon, ma'am?" the Texas Ranger said.

"You heard me, you moron! Arrest him!"

"Arrest who, ma'am?"

"Hiram Dalrymple! That's him with the neatly trimmed regimental-type brush mustache."

"Now, what would a poor, crazy west Texas rancher be doing dressed up like an Englishman and riding around in the Neiman-Marcus courtesy car?" the Texas Ranger asked reasonably. "But now that you mention it, ma'am, there is an all-points bulletin out for a lady fitting *your* description."

"What do you mean, *my* description?" Ida-Sue screamed.

"I got it right here," the Texas Ranger said, taking out his copy of the Teletype and reading aloud from it: 'The sort of cheap peroxide-blonde hussy who would trifle with a poor old man's affections.' That fits you to a T, lady," the ranger said. "Grab her, Slim, and put the cuffs on her!"

"Here's my card, honey," Hot Lips said. "When they let you out, look me up. It's never too late to change your ways, you know."

"Uncle Hiram!" Ida-Sue cried in desperation. "You're not going to let them do this to me, are you? To your very own niece? The mother of Scarlett?"

Uncle Hiram took the Corona cigar out from under his neatly trimmed regimental mustache. He sadly shook his head and then gestured, almost regally, with the cigar for the Rangers to take her away.

"Sorry to bother you folks with our dirty laundry," the Texas Ranger said.

"Think nothing of it," Hot Lips said.

"Enjoy the game," the ranger said, waving the Rolls into the parking lot.

There already was activity in the Texas Rangers' mobile disaster command post when word came in that the long arm of the law had finally been wrapped around the cheap peroxide-blonde hussy.

Fat Jack Stewing, M.D., F.A.S.P.P., raised the ten-gallon hat off the head of the taller of the two men suspended between two large Texas Rangers.

"This is obviously the chap we've been looking for," he said. "He's visibly quite mad."

"I tell you that I'm the Honorable Vibrato Val Vishnefsky, member of Congress," the fellow protested. "Tell him, Tiny Tony!"

"He's the Honorable Vibrato Val Vishnefsky!" Tiny Tony bellowed. "Member of Congress!"

"Of course he is," Fat Jack Stewing said. "Put the tall one in the straitjacket, officers, and dump him in the ambulance."

"What do we do with the short, fat one?"

"You have your orders," Richard Crochet, Attorney and Counselor at Law, said sternly. "Throw him into the slammer until he sobers up, and then turn him loose after a stern warning about aiding and abetting loonies on the run in the Great State of Texas."

At that point, the word came in about the apprehension of the cheap peroxide-blonde hussy. Wallington T. Dowd ordered that she be locked up with the short, fat guy, and then turned over to Dr. Stewing and Lawyer Crochet.

"That just about wraps it up, boys," Wally said with quiet pride, "except for the crazy Indian. And I just got word that they have him surrounded at the Bud-weiser stand. He was attempting to make off with a keg of beer."

"What seems to be the problem? Why haven't they arrested him?" Richard Crochet said.

"There seems to be a little misunderstanding," Wally Dowd confessed. "It's between my rangers and Green Beret Post 5660, V.F.W., but we hope to have it straightened out just as soon as the national guardsmen can get there." He paused, then explained: "We have the National Guard Green Beret Company helping us out today. They're nearly as good as my own rangers."

If the end of the "misunderstanding" had really depended on the arrival of the National Guard Green Beret Company, it would have been a long time in coming, for the commanding officer, in order to prepare his men for the ordeal of dealing with Green Beret Post 5660, V.F.W., had ordered his men to take a couple of hours of absolute rest before entering battle.

But it wasn't the national guardsmen who brought the affray to a conclusion; it was C. Bromwell Fosdick of the Secret Service. Just as soon as Texas Stadium came into view, Mr. Fosdick had climbed on top of his car, so as to have a better vantage point.

It was from that vantage point that, as soon as they rolled into the parking lot, he saw the disturbance at the Budweiser stand.

"You were right, Lenny," Fosdick called out. "His Royal Highness has changed disguises. Now he's dressed as an Indian."

As he rolled toward the battle scene, the Rolls-Royce carrying Hot Lips, and now Scarlett, Bubba, Hawkeye and Trapper John, as well, rolled majestically toward the battle scene from the other direction. Hot Lips really hadn't wanted to interfere, but the only way she could talk Uncle Hiram, who had kept his Colt-.45 single-action revolver, out of going himself was to give him her word that she would get Sitting Buffalo out of trouble.

"Come on, Hawkeye," she said.

"What for? I hardly know the guy!"

"He did give us the bubbly," Trapper John reminded him. "And he was out getting us some more firewater when they spotted him."

"You're right, of course," Hawkeye said. "Greater love hath no man than to battle the law to bring bubbly to his pals. I cannot refuse."

With flashing lights and screaming sirens, however, clearing a path for them, the stalwarts of the Secret Service reached the Budweiser stand first. Blowing on his little sterling silver whistle, and holding his official credentials out before him, C. Bromwell Fosdick forced his way through the battlers.

"Your Royal Highness," he said, "I'm dreadfully sorry for this terrible scene."

"Up yours, White Man!" Sitting Buffalo said, throwing a Texas Ranger into the beer cooler.

"That's him!" C. Bromwell Fosdick said. "He said the same thing to me in Spruce Harbor, Maine."

He had very little success in stopping the fight, however. Every time one of the Texas Rangers obeyed his stern orders to "cease and desist" and lowered his guard, he was decked by a member of Green Beret Post 5660, V.F.W.

At that point, the GILIAFCC, Inc., buses bearing the a cappella choir turned into the parking lot. Brother Lester spotted the Reverend Mother Emeritus standing on top of the Neiman-Marcus courtesy car.

"Yoo-hoo, Reverend Mother!" he called. "We're here! Yoo-hoo!"

The a cappella choir, in their lavender-and-yellow robes, debused, as they say, and started toward the scene.

For the first time in the long and proud history of the men of the Green Berets, they broke and ran in the midst of battle.

"Well," Bubba said to Scarlett, "there goes another cherished belief, shot to hell!"

"I'll do what I can, darling," Scarlett said, "to make it easy for you to bear." She handed Hawkeye Teddy Roosevelt's rope, and Hawkeye led Teddy Roosevelt into Texas Stadium to see the game.